# PERMANENT
# TOURISTS

Also by Genni Gunn

FICTION

*Solitaria*
*Hungers*
*Tracing Iris*
*On the Road*
*Thrice Upon a Time*

POETRY

*Faceless*
*Mating in Captivity*

NON-FICTION

*Tracks: Journeys in Time and Place*

TRANSLATIONS

*Devour Me Too*
*Travelling in the Gait of a Fox*
*Text Me*

OTHER

*Alternate Visions* (libretto)

# PERMANENT TOURISTS

## GENNI GUNN

EDITIONS

Cover design by Doowah Design.
Photo of Genni Gunn by Tom Hawkins

This book was printed on Ancient Forest Friendly paper.
Printed and bound in Canada by Hignell Book Printing Inc.

We acknowledge the support of the Canada Council for the Arts and the Manitoba Arts Council for our publishing program.

**Library and Archives Canada Cataloguing in Publication**

Title: Permanent tourists / Genni Gunn.
Names: Gunn, Genni, author.
Description: Short stories.
Identifiers: Canadiana (print) 20200319337 |
Canadiana (ebook)20200319345 |
ISBN 9781773240800 (softcover) |
ISBN 9781773240817 (HTML)

Classification: LCC PS8563.U572 P47 2020 | DDC
C813/.54—dc23

Signature Editions
P.O. Box 206, RPO Corydon, Winnipeg, Manitoba, R3M 3S7
www.signature-editions.com

# CONTENTS

*...See them. Men are always
Going somewhere.*

—from Maya Angelou, "Men"

*One could argue that those who have
abandoned their homes do not deserve
to live there and enjoy them.*

—José Saramago

# BEACHED

Panic never leaves her. It only recedes for intervals, like the tide in Bahía de Navidad. For days, the ocean laps in benign ripples on the sand, then suddenly rises in swirling breakers that smash to shore, shaking the hotel on its foundation. Monica lies in the penthouse bedroom facing the ocean, trying to force herself upright. It's a vacation, the waves a sea of mirrors reflecting the sun. Already children splash in the pool below, their stridor drilling into her brain.

"Mommy," Robbie cries, as he leaps on the bed, startling her. "There's a whale on the beach."

"A whale?" Monica smiles at him in his Mickey Mouse pyjamas. "Are you sure?" She drops her head on the pillow and closes her eyes. From across the way, the hotel owner's parrot lets out a wolf whistle, soft and sexy, each note drawn out. Then a series of cluck, cluck, clucks and chirps and whoops. She visualizes him in his large black cage, his green feathers clipped. From below, a rhythmic sweep of a broom on the outdoor hallways and stairs, a perpetual sound in the daylight hours.

"Mommy." Denise stands in the doorway, her pink/blue bathing suit an iridescent mermaid's skin. Already the boys have begun to take notice. She stares at Monica, her expression anxious. A camera hangs around her neck, nestled between her breasts like a third eye.

"It's true, Mommy." Robbie takes her hand and pulls. "Come see."

"Where's Daddy?" Monica says. "Show Daddy the whale. Mommy wants to rest a little more." She closes her eyes. For months now, she has been moving through the days as if in quicksand. If it were not for the children, whose needs force her to make breakfasts and lunches and dinners, to help with their homework and clean their clothes, if it were not for the children, whom she loves fiercely and wholeheartedly, she would have simply gone to bed long ago, and never gotten up. Where is Adrian, anyway? It's so like him to put this silly whale idea in the child's mind, then go off and leave her to deal with it.

Robbie's fascination with whales began two weeks ago, when one beached itself off the west coast of Vancouver Island. On TV, rescue workers poured seawater over the scorched grey flesh, spoke about sunburn and dehydration. It reminded Monica of another TV story in which a woman was found dead on a lounge chair, poolside in Vegas. She'd fallen asleep in the sun — six hours in 108 degrees — while all around her children and swimmers and sunbathers skirted her red, blistered body. Monica stared at the stranded whale on TV, tears streaming down her cheeks, while Adrian patiently explained to Robbie that whales have emotions, and can beach themselves out of grief and loneliness.

"I'm going down to the pool," Denise says. She turns and pads away, her bare feet making slapping sounds on the ceramic tile.

"Daddy's gone fishing with Travis," Robbie says, accusingly.

Monica sighs, a part of her relieved. Perhaps away from them all, Adrian and the boy can come to some understanding. "Maybe later Daddy will take you fishing too."

Robbie scrunches his eyebrows together. "But what can *I* do?" he says.

She closes her eyes and leans back onto the pillows, *But what can I do?* circling in her head.

"Mommy." Robbie pulls on her arm, and she winces, slowly sits up. Overnight, it seems, her chest and arms have turned an alarming flaming red. Yesterday, after a whispered argument with Adrian, she walked the forty-five minutes to Barra de Navidad along the length of the beach, without hat or sunscreen. She fingers her shoulders — already they're beginning to blister.

"Does it hurt?" Robbie says, lightly stroking his hand along her lower arm.

"It'll be fine." She embraces him and kisses him repeatedly in the side of his neck while he wriggles and struggles until they are both laughing.

"Come see," he says. She lets him pull her out of the bed. Together, they go to the veranda.

When a furious tide rolls in, small fish rise on the waves and land on wet sand. Pelicans circle overhead like wartime bombers, diving at the first sign of silver flapping on land. The air is black with wings, like a scene out of Hitchcock's *The Birds,* or Coppola's *Apocalypse Now* — helicopters whirling to *Ride of the Valkyries.* Monica steps into this dark moving sky, whose shadows projected, magnify on sand. Below, at the right corner of the courtyard, near the outdoor barbeque, Adrian and Travis stand together. Although only fourteen, Travis is as tall as his father, his body gangly like Adrian's was before he gained thirty pounds. Monica watches them anxiously for signs of trouble, but today, father and son are bent over the ceramic counter and sink, dark heads together, their hands black and wet.

"Hey!" she calls. "What are you doing?"

"We've caught an octopus," Adrian says, holding out an inky squishy pulp.

Denise darts across the courtyard, camera at her eye. "Hold it," she says and snaps a photograph.

Adrian frowns at her.

"Sorry," she says. "Relevant narrative." She smiles and caps the lens. For the past six months, Denise, who is thirteen-going-on-thirty, has been snapping these "relevant narratives," developing them, and pasting them into a scrapbook, which she calls the storyboard of her life. Although Adrian has bought her the latest Canon camcorder, Denise prefer stills, which nobody sees because she has rigged a small padlock on the scrapbook. Monica wonders how these narratives will fare through the years. Will they resemble memories, sanitized or demonized at will?

Robbie tugs at Monica's hand. "Let's go down, Mommy. I want to touch the octopus too." His voice is reverent, excited, the whale forgotten. He's four, and his father is a hazy memory, having recently returned after an eighteen-month absence, which he and Monica explained to the children as an overseas posting. Adrian is a marine biologist, and often away on field work — "field work" that includes lovers — so the children are accustomed to his absences. But Monica suspects Denise and Travis sense that Adrian's latest omission from their lives was due to problems between him and her, problems which although the children never heard about, they could see in the askance glances of their parents, feel in the icy tightening around their hearts.

"Don't lock the door," Travis calls out. "I'm coming up to put the octopus in the fridge." Monica watches them slide the creature in a pail, watches Adrian stride out the gate to the concrete terrace at the front of the hotel.

That *was* a relevant moment, she thinks, a rare occasion with Adrian and Travis appearing — at least in the storyboard — as if they were united. It reminds her of the last photo, the one Denise took of them two weeks ago while they were building a tackle box — Adrian's choice for Travis's grade nine woodworking project. What is not visible in that photo is that Travis wanted to build a chess table or a bookshelf, but his father considers these unsuitable and unnecessary objects for a young man he thinks spends far too much time reading novels when he should be outside playing sports and doing boy things. The relevant narratives, Monica thinks, are the ones you don't see, the photographs in the mind's eye — your husband and his lover in restaurants, theatres, movies, airplanes. How did it happen, she wonders. *What can I do?*

Adrian and Travis built the tackle box to bring here with them to Mexico. They are in Obregón, a small village north of Manzanillo, booked into the most modern, albeit most expensive hotel in the village. It rises out of the sand like a fairy castle, all turrets and domes, some of which are penthouse bedrooms, others decorative covers for water reservoirs and laundry facilities. Each of the four floors has three apartments, and a wraparound covered veranda large enough for individual tables and chairs. At night, Monica cooks dinner, then she, Adrian and the children eat off blue-and-white Talavera plates set on madras tablecloths. After supper, Travis and Denise escape to the village with a pack of teenagers they met two days into their holiday. Monica and Adrian play Go Fish with Robbie until his bedtime, then, tumblers and blender of margaritas in hand, they join other couples downstairs in the courtyard and drink around the pool until the children return.

The holiday is half pleasure, half business, a perk paid for by Adrian's prospective boss Chester Fowler, who, along with his wife Heather, joined them a few days after their arrival. Monica is not thrilled with this arrangement, viewing it as a test for which she has not studied.

Robbie stares after his father, toward the beach. "I told you, Mommy," he says, and for a moment, he looks like Adrian smirking at Monica over something. "Look. There. It's a whale."

The large blubbery mass does indeed resemble a whale. Sunlight reflects off pale blue jeans and fa aded blue-checked shirt, so that it forms a silvery shape on dry sand, inches above the high tide mark.

"It's a man," Monica says, thinking how easily reflections distort the senses. "I hope he's all right." She goes inside, changes into shorts and shirt, slips into her flip-flops, and the two of them head downstairs. They pass Travis on the landing, but Robbie is now too excited about the whale to care about the octopus.

"Could he be a man-whale?" Robbie says. "Like a mermaid, only a man."

"I don't think so." Monica ducks at the second landing where the ceiling is not quite high enough for her to clear the top stair.

"Is he dead then?" Robbie says. "Was he sad?"

"Let's wait till we see him, all right?" Surely all of them out there have seen the man. She takes Robbie's hand and together they cross the luxurious courtyard, past the swimming pool, past the hibiscus, banana plants and palms, past the outdoor barbeque area, past the gate onto the terrace overlooking the ocean, where hotel guests are settled on chairs and loungers, their flesh oiled and sunscreened, turning in the sun, like hogs on a spit.

Adrian and Chester slouch in deck chairs, a plastic table between them on which two bottles of Estrella weep round wet pools. They're playing poker. This is the new Adrian she can't quite reconcile to the marine biologist who patiently explains the complex lives of fish to Robbie and Denise, the Adrian who used to help Travis write essays about the fragile balance of the seas' ecology. This past year, Adrian has worked on an international research project with several oil companies to explore the ocean's depths, at the end of which Chester approached him with a job offer. No, she can't reconcile this man, her husband, grappled into his prospective boss's power.

On the beach below, the man lies on his side, legs together, one arm straight out, supporting his large dark head, his hips a mountain in the centre of his sloping body, his feet together, the black toes of his shoes turned out like tail flukes. Flotsam and seaweed are scattered about him, collected in the folds of his clothes, embedded in the crevices of his flesh. She wonders if he is someone she has spoken to, bartered with, if he has walked this stretch of beach day after day, a carapace of T-shirts, hammocks, jewellery and masks on his back.

"Good morning, Monica," Chester says when he sees her. "Another lovely day in paradise." He laughs, as if he has said something witty and original. His wife, Heather, raises her head and laughs uproariously, her book pressed against her chest, the cover of which shows a sun setting over a placid lake. NORA ROBERTS takes up one third of the page.

Monica nods, then looks at Adrian. "What's the matter with him?" she says, indicating the man on the sand. "He's not —"

"Passed out drunk," Adrian says, and raises his beer. Chester picks his up, and clinks bottles, toasting…what? Monica wonders. "No need to worry," Adrian says. He and Chester return to their card game, and Heather to her book.

Monica stands, uncertain, staring at the Mexican man, whose face she suddenly recognizes. Last night, the four of them had been drinking around the pool when they heard a commotion on the beach. Monica had gotten up and walked out past the gate to the edge of the terrace, heard voices and the muffled sound of children. Beside her, several couples were playing cards, while others stared at the beach as if it were live theatre.

"What's going on?" Monica had asked.

One of the men shrugged. "Some kind of Mexican thing. Cheers," he said, raising his Estrella.

Monica had gone down the four stairs to the sand, and away from the artificial lights, her eyes took in the flicker of flashlights. It seemed the whole village was here, lined up along the high tide mark, stretching across the horizon in front of her. She walked down to where a group of men and women stood among dozens of buckets. "What's going on?" she'd asked again.

"Turtle release," a tall young woman said. "Leatherbacks. Endangered." She explained that various species of sea turtles come to this coast in search of warm sand, where they lay their eggs. When the baby turtles emerge from their shells, they have to reach the water — a dangerous feat for such tiny creatures. "We help them," the young woman said. Three hundred baby turtles squirmed in buckets, waiting to be set on waves in darkness so that birds wouldn't eat them. And even then, only a tiny percentage would survive the ocean's trials.

"Adrian," Monica called once, twice, "you've got to see this!"

He set his drink down and came towards her, his lips tight. However, as soon as he saw the buckets on the beach, he grew animated, as if the turtles had jolted him into his former self. "Let's get Robbie," he said, and they ran upstairs together and woke Robbie. Carried him down to the water's edge. The Mexican man who now lies on the beach had gently placed two hatchlings into Robbie's hands, showed him how to set the wriggling turtles on wet sand. Black creatures scrambled toward the ocean like wound-up toys, beckoned by the beach's downslide, the white peaks of waves, the chiaroscuro at the horizon, and on reaching the water, they swam in a frenzy, while Adrian's soft voice explained about nature, the cruelty of it.

Now, in the hot sun, it seems impossible that they were here, last night, on this same hard sand where this man who now lies beached cupped delicate hatchlings in his large hands; on this same sand, where Adrian was a different man.

She stares at the closed eyes, the hair tousled over his cheek. He'll get sunstroke, she thinks, touching her own pink cheeks. Fortunately, at the moment, his shoulders create shade for his head. "How long has he been there?" she asks.

Heather looks up from her book. She peers at Monica, smug. "It's disgraceful," she says, crossing her legs at the ankles.

Monica frowns, wondering what she means. It's disgraceful that he's been there so long? That no one has done anything to help? She stares at Heather, whose enormous black sunglasses resemble a stingray perched on her nose. On the terrace, Adrian is tense, leaning forward, face tight, signalling Monica with the narrowing of his eyes. She stares at the thick paperback Heather has laid face-down on her lap, and is now pressing, breaking the spine. She makes herself think of PTA meetings, softball games and high-school pageants; she makes herself think of Robbie's incantation every night, "Please God, keep Daddy safe so he can come home," of Travis and Denise, who wear their longing in their curved shoulders, in the hard edges of their blue eyes.

Heather pats a lawn chair next to her, and Monica sits down. Travis, who has come downstairs, sits at the edge of the concrete, legs swinging over the four-foot drop, fishing pole planted in the sand, eyes fixed straight ahead.

Monica has disliked Chester and Heather Fowler since they arrived, disliked their disparaging of everything Mexican, the condescending smiles they give her when she disagrees with them, the types of statements like the one Heather made. For four days, Monica has been choking on her words, while Adrian sits, comfortable, his large hands constantly in motion, his lips stretched into smiles, his body thrust anxiously towards theirs. She knows it's no good between her and Adrian, that he's only back for a while, that his affair soured. He's a tourist here in their lives, and yet when she thinks of him permanently gone, her throat constricts and her heart palpitates until she's sure it will leap out of her chest.

"Is it a whale-man?" Robbie asks.

Chester guffaws.

"Aren't you cute," Heather says. "Yes, you're right, it's a kind of animal." She smiles.

Robbie looks at them, unsure, but pleased that they're all beaming at him. "A whale is not an animal," he says, puffing up like a blowfish. "It's a mammal."

"We're all mammals, honey," Heather says. "But some of us are more mammals than others." She shrieks with laughter, and Adrian and Chester howl along, although Monica can make no sense out of her statement.

Travis glowers at them all, gets up and marches, stone-faced, down the beach. Monica watches him go, a flapping of wings in her heart, magnifying black.

"Oh look!" Chester says to Robbie. "Your whale is moving. Maybe it'll get right back into the ocean where it belongs." He points to the man, whose leg is slowly bending at the knee. At each movement, he and Heather and Adrian hoot and whoop, as if the man were performing a circus act for their amusement.

"It's not really a whale," Robbie says then.

"Of course it is, honey," Heather insists, patting his arm. "It's doing tricks for us, can't you see?"

Robbie glances at Monica, who begins to shake her head, but Adrian snaps his fingers and Robbie turns to his father, who smiles and nods.

Monica glares at Adrian and gets up. She'll go to the lobby and see what can be done for the man. Denise is sitting by the pool, sleek and wet, eyes curious. *She has been watching and listening to us*, Monica thinks. Denise observes everything, and is a chameleon. In a room of people, Denise has the uncanny ability to say exactly what each person wants to hear. Monica feels a fist pressing against her abdomen. She wants to say, *I'm here, I'm here, I'll always be here*. Waves merrily instead.

In the lobby, two young men are tacking a glittery sign — WELCOME TO THE YEAR 2000! — above the front desk. One of them points to a signup sheet for a Millennial Party. Monica shakes her head, and uses a combination of English and broken Spanish. Then, frustrated by her inability to communicate clearly, she mimes the man on the beach.

"The policemen will take him away. Soon, don't worry," the desk clerk says, misunderstanding her motive. She tries to explain, then gives up; smiles and shakes her head instead.

In front of the hotel, the beached man moves in slow motion, like an octopus out of water. An elaborate dance — he draws up one knee, his elbow slides in the sand, a finger crooks, his nose twitches, his foot wiggles. The Fowlers point to him and laugh whenever he moves. Robbie is sitting on Adrian's lap, his face flushed and excited. Monica feels her stomach tighten again. "Robbie," she calls from across the courtyard, but he doesn't hear her.

She knows she should do something. Take the children and board a plane home. Pack, find an apartment. Go back to work. It's been fifteen years since she was a graduate student. She could

re-enroll and finish her anthropology degree. She could…
she could…her head swarms with a multitude of options that
exhaust her.

On the sand, the man grimaces. Monica wonders what griefs
have propelled him here, on this stretch of beach to be dissected
by hard, impassive eyes. Where are his wife and family? Has
someone died?

Denise has moved her lawn chair to the terrace. Monica
watches her inch closer to her father. In and out. Back and
forth. Adrian has been the perfect gift bearer: bikes, skates,
pointe shoes, flute, piano, soccer ball, camcorder, computers,
laptops, cellphones, iPods, iPads, CDs, DVDs. And when he's
away, only she notices the children quickening when the phone
rings. *Be careful*, she wants to say, watching Robbie and Denise
near their father's riptide love.

"Oh, honey," Heather says, "we can't let that alabaster skin
get tough now, can we?" She motions Denise into the lawn
chair beside her, laughs, reaches into her bag, and pulls out
sunscreen, which she spreads on Denise's arms and back.
"When I was your age," she says, in a southern US drawl, "My
mother never let me out in the sun without a hat."

· Monica bristles. She huffs over to them. "Perhaps that's
because you lived in Arizona," she says. "In Vancouver were we
live, we mostly get rain — "

"Mu-um," Denise says in a please-be-quiet-and-don't-
embarrass-us-all tone.

They are all staring at her as if they are the family, and she is
the outsider. She turns away, then curls herself into a deck chair
a little apart from them, scanning the shore: she can barely
discern Travis walking steadily away from them. Her heartbeat
quickens, and she makes herself count, to keep the panic away. If
only she had a book, a crossword puzzle, something to distract
her. For a moment, she considers going up the four flights of
stairs to their penthouse rooms, but she resists, aware of the
domino effect: once there, she would sink into bed and sleep
the rest of the day; then Adrian would be furious — "What kind

of wife goes on vacation and stays in bed all day?" — and she'd respond with "What kind of husband abandons his wife and three children for a fuck?" And he'd have to defend his ex-lover, and accuse Monica of not being capable of forgiveness, and she would retort that forgiveness could only be given once, not twice for the same sin, and the quarrel would continue ad infinitum, almost word for word, as it had for the past month, since his return. No, it's better to stay here, she thinks, calming herself. She moves her chair into the partial shade of the pergola.

In the distance, finally, a dune buggy. And soon, a policeman bends over the sleeping man, shakes him, all in vain. He looks up at them, and Monica thinks they must look like an amateur theatre troupe, splayed out on the terrace, callous and indifferent. She rises out of the deck chair, and jumps off the platform onto the white, hot sand.

Denise begins to follow, camera in hand, but Heather pulls her firmly down. "You stay here, honey," she says.

Chester sets his beer on the plastic table, gets up, and stomps down the three steps, yelling at the policeman, hands waving in the air. "This is our beach. We've paid good money for it. Get him out of there."

The policeman hardly glances at the gesticulating man, his eyes scornful.

Monica bites her lip. "I'm sorry," she murmurs, head motioning toward the group on the pad.

The policeman's cold stare bores through her, and she flushes. He turns the beached man over gently, checks his pulse, tries to lift him, but can't.

No one offers to help.

"They're all the same, really," Heather says. "Back home, they're lying on the sidewalks."

"I wouldn't stand for it if this was my hotel," Chester mutters, climbing back onto the terrace. He yanks a beer out of his personal cooler and flips off the cap with the opener attached to his keys.

"Well, it's not your hotel," Monica says. "And it's not your country." She climbs up on the platform.

Both Denise and Adrian stiffen.

"Monica is not herself today," Adrian says. "She got sunburned yesterday, and now she's cranky." He laughs. "Come here, darling," he says, and pulls her down into a deck chair beside him.

Denise looks for her reaction, camera poised. *This is the relevant narrative*, Monica wants to say. *All that's not said.* She stares at the sleeping man, envious of his oblivion, imagines herself lying down next to him, awaiting the tide.

The policeman arranges the man on his side, away from the sun. "I will be back with help," he says to the audience collected on the terrace, and drives off, wheels spitting out sand. Monica shades her eyes and stares after him. In the distance, Travis's body shrinks smaller and smaller.

Adrian reaches out and squeezes her hand.

"Daddy, look!" Robbie says. He runs to the edge of the concrete and jumps off. Unbuttoned, his shirt puffs in the air like a carapace. Adrian and Monica and the Fowlers applaud. He scurries up the stairs and does it again, and again, while they beam and clap and laugh. Denise pulls out her camera. Both children are bright-eyed, in love.

Then Robbie plucks the fishing pole out of the sand. He runs to the beached man, plants the pole at his head and stands there, triumphant.

"How marvellous!" Heather squeals. "You've got yourself a whale."

"Moby Dick," Adrian says. Robbie doesn't know what this means, but he is drunk with the admiration in his father's voice.

Denise grabs her camera and hops onto the sand. "Look at me, Daddy," she says, her voice tight, framing Robbie and the man in the viewfinder. Before she takes the photo, she turns for a moment toward Adrian, toward his wide toothy grin.

*Grief is like the ocean;*
*it comes on waves ebbing and flowing.*
*Sometimes the water is calm,*
*and sometimes it is overwhelming.*
*All we can do is learn to swim.*

—Vicki Harrison

# SOLITUDES

Although it was a clear and sunny day, no people gathered on the rich green grass, no children's pockets filled with pebbles. No men shifted from foot to foot, no women gossiped. There was no pyramid of stones, no big black box.

The man sat cross-legged on a patch of earth, on the russet bank of what appeared to be a lake, but was a moat 200 metres wide. He was in his mid-thirties and wore a faded crimson shirt, sleeves rolled up, and blue jeans. His feet were bare. Pond herons wafted in the air in long smooth glides to the surface of still water. Behind the man, a boy splashed waist-deep, collecting pink and purple water lilies. Across the gravel road, an array of vendor stands shimmered in the heat, kaleidoscopic with silk scarves and purses in reds, oranges, and purples, stone amulets to ward off evil, postcards and guidebooks, and rows and rows of water-colour Brahmas who stared out with stony eyes. The man could have been a tourist, a bas-relief against Angkor Wat's quincunx pediments, which rose into a sun-lit sky; a tourist resting, perhaps, in the shade of a banyan tree after a day's trekking through temples, but for the large black plastic bag which lay beside him open and overflowing with empty water bottles.

Vivian saw him first, as she and Freda rounded a corner, fanning themselves with cultural travel guides, their hair semi-plastered to their heads, their feet sluggish in sports sandals, as they searched for the rental car and driver who had dropped them off at dawn. They were both in their late twenties, childhood friends who had survived the divide of university and of different career paths. Vivian worked as a naturopath in a wellness clinic, and Freda as a receptionist for a revolving door of employers. They had been in Cambodia for four days, exploring the recently proclaimed Eighth Wonder of the World, Angkor Wat, the seat of the Khmer Empire when Cambodia was at its height; Angkor Wat, the world's largest religious structure, and the only religious monument to appear on a national flag. Birds circled above them, landed in the banyans and *kapots* whose tubular, aerial roots fell and spread like white hair.

Poised in a wide semi-circle around the man were four teenage boys in jeans and T-shirts. One wore a light windbreaker. They could have been playing a game, so cheerful they were, as each stooped, picked up a stone and hurled it at the man, whose arms rose up, whose hands tried to protect his face. The rocks hammered the man's head, his chest, his arms, and legs.

"Stop that!" Vivian said, dashing toward them. "What do you think you're doing?"

The boys turned, startled, then seeing her, laughed, and continued to pelt the man. She stamped her foot, waved her arms, yelling. One of the boys grew more vicious, assumed a pitcher's wind-up pose, for better, harder aim. The stone cut a welt into the man's forehead. Blood seeped into his eyebrow.

"Come on," Freda said, tugging at Vivian's elbow. "Let's just go."

Vivian shook her off with an incredulous look.

Across the street, two shopkeepers emerged from the canopy of their stands. The younger one opened a yellow umbrella against the sun. On seeing the man, they quickly bent to pick up stones. Vivian stood in their path. "Stop! Stop!" she said to the two women. "Are you all crazy?"

The shopkeepers stared at her, frowning. The boys turned to the new scene, stones in hand. One of them said, "*He* crazy," nodding to the man. The boy's black T-shirt read MEGADETH in red letters above a nuclear explosion.

"He's hurt," Vivian said. She walked towards the man, and took a tissue from her fanny pack, intending to dab the trickle of blood on his forehead.

The man shrank from her, shaking his head. His arms covered his face. He began to wail. The boys laughed and circled him in a crazy dance. Vivian felt light-headed; she began to hear a soundtrack of parakeets, parrots, cicadas, all chattering, a soundtrack of strident clickings and buzzings. She turned her head, trying to make out the words. Closed her eyes. *The bones cry out... the flesh calls for blood.*

"What?" Freda asked.

Vivian opened her eyes. Had she spoken or had he? "That man... ," she said and bit her lip. "That's what...he's saying."

Freda stared at her curiously. "You don't know Cambodian, Vivian. The man is not saying anything. He's crying."

"But I'm sure I heard..." Vivian looked at the man, who was now curved into a ball, his head low on his chest, his arms wildly trying to deflect the stones. Hadn't she? Her half-sister Marissa's face swam up before her eyes, disembodied and smiling. *I will not do this*, Vivian said to herself. *I will not.* She took a few deep breaths.

One of the boys mimicked her. "*Bone cry out*," he said, advancing, eyes wide and mocking. "*Flesh call blood.*" He raised his arm and she flinched.

"He possessed," one of the shopkeepers said. "No soul." She picked up another stone, and threw it half-heartedly, so that it did not reach the man, who moaned and moved his head from side to side in a wanton rhythm.

"There's something wrong with him," Vivian said. Japanese encephalitis, she thought. All those rice paddies and pigs. Could that have affected his brain? Or war. Or torture. Or family.

The shopkeeper stepped back, as if Vivian had struck her. She shook her head. "He my teacher once," she said. "But now *preay*...evil spirit..." She undid the knot in her rainbow batik-marbled *sampot*, rearranged and reknotted it around her slim waist. Then she turned and walked to her stand. The other followed, looking back furtively only once from beneath the yellow umbrella.

"What about karma?" Vivian called after them. "That could be you in a next life."

The shopkeepers continued walking. Vivian turned to the boys.

"This *his* karma," one said. He shrugged and picked up a stone.

*Sticks and stones will break my bones…* What of these people, stone-faced, stone-blind, stone-hearted? Were their convictions solid as rocks? Left long enough, stones age to gems and guard against affection. Held in the hand, a stone is a conscience. Was their fear a good-neighbour fence or a prison wall? Vivian trudged slowly to the parking lot, trying to understand the incomprehensible, her feet raising red puffs of dust. Freda followed behind her, texting the stoning in vivid detail to her girlfriends in Toronto. Vivian drew out her own cellphone, checked for missed calls or messages, but there were none. Where was Marissa? Why hadn't she called?

o o o

Marissa stepped into the air-conditioned charter plane, the heat and humidity of Mexico clinging to her skin. She strapped herself into her seat beside a young couple returning home after an all-inclusive holiday, the girl's hair braided in cornrows, the boy's muscle shirt damp against his chest. All around her, revellers whooped and laughed, bodies squeezed into halters and bikini tops, shorts and sandals, as if they were flying to another tropical destination instead of to Vancouver in January.

The plane taxied along the shoreline, and Marissa stared out the window at the white sand of Playa de Oro and the treacherous ocean waves where, according to the onboard magazine *¡Fiesta!*, in 1862, a ship carrying gold coins had burned, and more than 200 of its passengers and crew had drowned trying to get to shore. She clasped her hands together on her lap. She was not afraid of flying, only of *oceans, lakes, rivers, streams, brooks, lagoons, basins, lochs, pools.*

As the plane rose, the ocean formed a postcard of turquoise peaks, its dangers invisible under the surface. She wondered about the countless dead in its depths. Had they been ferried across the river Styx? Used the gold coins for passage? Drunk from the water of the Lethe? Had they forgotten what they'd done, who they were? How they'd suffered? She leaned back into her seat and thought about her mother stowed in a coffin below. *Safe passage, Mother.*

Two weeks before, her mother had been packing in an upstairs bedroom at home, pleading with Marissa to change her mind and accompany her to Mexico. She had tried everything from bribes to guilt, but for once, Marissa had not succumbed. She had told her mother that she was not willing to spend three weeks stuffed into a bus with a load of blue-haired pensioners in SAS shoes, when the truth was that her mother's insistence that they return to Mexico after all that had happened there left Marissa unsettled and alarmed. Her mother had cajoled, cried and moped, but Marissa would not relent. Her mother was barely sixty, a grim, determined woman. Since the death of her husband, her distress manifested in various vague and non-diagnosable illnesses, a woman who, Marissa felt, could manage without her.

"You're such a disappointment," her mother had said on the Skytrain to the airport, shaking her head in familiar martyrdom. Then with a small tight smile she had boarded the plane, and within days she was on the bus that crashed over a cliff on the Costa Careyes and left no survivors.

Marissa sighed. From her grey backpack, she drew out *The Lonely Passion of Judith Hearne,* a deliciously depressing novel, and a black velveteen neck pillow she had bought at the Manzanillo airport. She inflated the pillow, put it around her neck and leaned back, eyes closed. The details of the past week flitted behind her lids, disordered and chaotic. Forms to sign, the crushed Golden Tours bus, the slashed purple Ultralight suitcase, her mother's blue marbled skin. She forced herself to think of the future instead. She would use the insurance money to pay off the mortgage on the house — a two-storey mock-Tudor, with gouged hardwood floors, bubbling paint, and shabby, lumpy wallpaper peeling from lath-and-plaster walls, a house that had fallen into ruin since her father died. She would be happy.

o o o

Vivian and Freda wound among the dozens of taxis and buses and tuk-tuks lined up and waiting for tourists eager for air conditioning and hotel showers. To Vivian's relief, the driver waved to them as they approached. How would they ever have located him otherwise? The monument was only accessible on foot, and they were part of a spurt of tourists streaming down the stone causeway a third of a mile long over the moat which had once been filled with crocodiles. They snaked past a row of open restaurants with palm-frond roofs and plastic tables and chairs, dodging restaurant workers' entreaties and vendors trying to sell them the identical guidebooks they held in their hands. A cow grazed on corn husks at one of the tables, beside a red plastic chair. A humungous blue bus narrowly missed them, but left in its wake a wall of coral dust. Two boys cycled past.

"Over here," Mr. San called. He held the door open for them. He had been their driver since their arrival, a mid-forties, attractive man with fine bones and a melancholy look in his bleached brown eyes, like a silent film star. Despite the heat, he looked fresh and unruffled in his black trousers and white shirt, unlike how Vivian felt in her white dusty capris and sweaty pink tank top. In the car, she took off her canvas hat and waved it in front of her face. A wisp of straight blonde hair stuck to one corner of her mouth. Mr. San handed them each a water bottle, then flicked on the air conditioning.

They drove out of the parking complex, past the man who still sat on the ground, a crowd clustered around him. "Why are they doing that?" Vivian said. "That poor man."

Mr. San glanced at the scene and shrugged. "Maybe he inherited bad luck. Or maybe," he said, fingering the *lingam* amulet around his throat, "he is possessed by *besach*."

"What's that?" Vivian asked.

"The spirit of person who have a violent death."

"There must be a lot of those around here," Freda said.

Vivian looked at him. "You live with this terrible past," she said, "and yet, you stone a man because you think he's crazy?" She shook her head.

"The man is crazy because a demon has taken him. It is too late for him. We must stone the demon before it comes inside us."

*Historical, this hunting and stoning of the possessed: easy release for our forbidden thoughts and desires. In the biblical tale, the possessed man had banished himself to a tomb, and spent his days crying out and pelting himself with stones so that he was permanently bruised and scarred. The villagers did not dare kill him, convinced the demons inside him were doing the stoning. They chained him repeatedly, put him in ankle irons, but the possessed easily broke out of all. And so all let him roam — they had a scapegoat, and the madman had his life.*

o o o

The dripping sounds began on Marissa's first night back. Intermittent, and maddeningly difficult to locate. *Drip…drip… drip…*It made her think *wet hair, gutters, hoses, irrigation, intravenous, torture, veins, guilt*. It sounded as if someone had not turned a faucet tight enough up in the attic, but there was no bathroom up there, only a series of rafters and two-by-sixes, between which lay pink discoloured insulation with mouse droppings in its creases.

Before her mother died, Marissa had been living here with her, in this house where she was born, in the room where, as a child, she'd travelled with imaginary friends to the faraway places inside her books. She had continued living here, at her mother's insistence, even when she was well enough to have applied for a part-time job, possibly at the bookstore. That first year following that disastrous Christmas and the breakdown of mind and home, she was embarrassed to have left school so suddenly, to have to explain to her friends. She needn't have worried, because before she knew it, five years had passed, and her high school friends had left for other cities, universities, marriages. Then two years ago, when her father died, Marissa's and her mother's roles reversed, and Marissa became the caretaker for a time. Often she felt panicky, unable to breathe, the shroud of her mother's sadness settled over her, and she'd call her half-sister Vivian in Toronto, who calmed her in a steady, sympathetic voice, who sent her money and advice. Marissa had had the odd boyfriend years ago, but her timidity had scared them off. Or so she had always thought. She wondered now if her mother had been responsible, or perhaps if what had frightened them was her own unconditional submission.

She was twenty-five, a pale, slender young woman of medium height, with dark curly hair and large brown eyes that flitted anxiously from thing to thing, from person to person, as if she were afraid to focus her attention. In a room full of people, she was unnoticed beneath the men's shirts and loose jeans she had taken to wearing. Her mother used to refer to her as "fragile," although Marissa knew what she really meant was something else.

The house would be an antidote to grief. Already, Marissa was planning the scraping and sanding, the hammering and sawing, the prepping and painting that would turn this house into her home. (She heard the drip, cocked her head, trying to locate the sound.) And if she ever got through every room, years of landscaping awaited in the tangled garden, from which she could see the ocean. She was fortunate to own this modest house in

Point Grey, nestled between two new monster homes, on a small lot that contained an easement, and thus could not be developed further. She was fortunate to have cheated death once again.

o  o  o

In the hotel room, while Freda showered, Vivian phoned Marissa in Vancouver, but reached a robotically cheerful female greeting. Vivian left one more message, yet another duplicate of countless duplicates she'd left over the past few days, its frequency in direct proportion to her growing anxiety. Her stomach felt queasy, and she reached into her purse for an antacid tablet. Then she lay on her back, fighting the vertigo that threatened to overwhelm her. She had not spoken to her half-sister since Marissa had called her two weeks before, her voice slurred and weepy, begging her to come to Vancouver, as if Vivian didn't have a job in Toronto, as if their father had not abandoned Vivian and her mother and started a second family when Vivian was only four. Marissa's voice had filled Vivian's voicemail with references to drips and coins and other nonsense. Vivian was sick of it, sick of listening to her sister's tales of woe, when she had a perfectly good house to live in, and now her mother's insurance money. Marissa was twenty-five, for god's sakes, and despite the fact that before his death, Vivian had promised her father to look out for her sister should anything happen, she heard herself say, "Try taking care of yourself for a change." She'd hung up, fully expecting Marissa would call her in a couple of days, when she was back to normal, although Vivian didn't know what exactly constituted "normal" for her sister. She hadn't heard from Marissa since.

She picked up her travel guide and leafed through it. The Khmer Temples rose in glossy splendour. Demons and deities, defiant, guarded the gates. Three-headed elephants. The turreted faces of Brahmas stared out of their cardinal points, seeing all. Laterite stacked into heads, furrowed and pocked by rain and wind. There was nothing about stoning.

"Tough love is good," Freda said later, when they were walking in the dark up a busy street to find a restaurant. "She's probably moving forward. Be happy about it."

But Vivian did not feel anything close to happiness. She didn't even feel relief that Marissa hadn't called and spoiled her holiday. Her sister was the boulder Vivian was condemned to roll uphill for an eternity. "I hope she's okay," she said. The early evening air hung heavy and humid. Vivian wished she'd worn a dress instead of her jeans. A viscous throng of cars, tuk-tuks and motorbikes clotted the street, their headlights like large fireflies in the dark. Hotel marquees announced *Aspara Dancing* or *Happy Hour*, or *Two for One Dinner Free*, signs glittering in multicoloured fairy lights. A motorbike veered towards them on the shoulder of the road. She and Freda stood still while it manoeuvred around them. Dust rose into their faces. Vivian was beginning to regret their decision to walk from the hotel. A tuk-tuk would have been much cleaner and safer.

"You did the right thing," Freda said. She brushed dust off her black dress. Unlike Vivian, she was wearing impossibly high sling-back heels that threatened to twist her ankle at every step. "I bet she pulled up her socks and is getting on with it." Motorbikes whizzed past them on the left, on the right, going in every direction.

"Maybe," Vivian said, unconvinced. They stopped at a traffic light and crossed onto a wide paving-stone sidewalk.

Over the past decade, Vivian had become accustomed to fielding Marissa's intermittent rambling calls and messages of appropriated sadness derived from books and TV stories — an unrequited love, a boat lost at sea, a dead character in a movie — as if she expected Vivian to solve something undefined. "I'm drowning," she'd wail, and Vivian would talk her down, thinking *wallowing* was more like it. She found it increasingly difficult to empathize and sympathize. Cry Wolf.

"She should have called and let me know she's okay," she said to Freda now, as they walked past a dilapidated guest house, a restaurant whose sign boasted *We Do Not Serve Monkey, Snake,*

*Rat or Dog*, then a right turn onto Sivatha Street, a main artery flanked with restaurants and shops.

They passed a vacant building whose front was plastered with ads for designer merchandise — Gucci shoes, Armani suits, Prada purses — all in multiple colours. A few doors down, a tiny internet café, squeezed between a bamboo papaya stand and a digital photo shop. A little further on, Freda stopped in front of a souvenir/naturopathic shop to admire crystals and stones carved into amulets and jewellery. "I love these," she said, pulling Vivian inside. "Let's pop in for a second and have a look."

Vivian smiled and let herself be guided in. Freda was a good friend; she was trying in her own way to distract Vivian, to keep her from obsessing about her sister, and doing so by appealing to Vivian's penchant for healing stones.

"Just the thing for you," Freda said, picking up a moonstone beside which was a card outlining its magical properties: *This stone will help psychic power and answer question in a dream.* "You can dream all about Marissa tonight." She paid for it, then handed it to Vivian, who turned it over and over in her hand, watching blue and rainbow flashes before zipping it into the pocket of her hoody.

"I hope not," Vivian said. She imagined a dream in which Marissa was wandering back alleys, dumpster-diving, doorway-slumbering under boarded, graffitied windows. Why couldn't Marissa keep a job for more than a month or two? Sure, she was moody, erratic. Vivian had spent countless hours and dollars speaking to her on the phone. She wished Marissa's mother were still alive. She'd know what to do. Or maybe she'd simply continue to do what Vivian now felt was a burden. *She needs help*, her mother had said. *Medication, maybe. I don't know. But she's not right.* Vivian refused to consider this as a possibility. Medication is for Americans, she thought. If she could get up at 7:00 a.m. every morning to go to work, so could her sister.

o o o

That first night, from her upstairs bedroom window, Marissa counted ocean liners in the harbour, lights aglow, like Christmas decorations hanging in darkness. She was alone in the house, unsupervised. The last time she had felt this unencumbered, she was sixteen, on holiday in Mexico with her parents, booked into a hotel in San Patricio, on a near-deserted stretch of beach where, each evening, when the adults gathered around the pool, drinks in hand, the teenagers roamed the back streets of the little village, their sandals raising clouds of dust. At night, in the oblong of their flashlights, the brilliant blooms of bougainvillea and hibiscus spilling over walls startled Marissa with their casual existence, not like at home, where nature was manicured and ordered. In the *zócalo*, they sat on the cool stone parapets and watched couples, clusters of girls, groups of boys, families in Sunday bests, all strolling around in a peacock parade, searching for friends and lovers, whispering among themselves. A trio played in the white gazebo at the centre of the *zócalo*, guitar riffs mingling with the cacophony of crickets, dogs barking, a car's security alarm beep beep beeping, with the myriad voices in the square. Marissa was drunk with the romance of it all, and so had easily fallen crazy in love for the first time, there one night, almost instantly, in the way teenagers are smitten, her hands trembling in her lap when the boy looked at her. He was seventeen, a dark, moody creature the girls gazed at from behind half-closed lids. She had felt *recognized,* and when he had reached for her hand and pulled her up amid the swirl of bodies, she had followed. From that breathless first meeting, she and the boy had been inseparable, as if they had always been severed halves and only now had become whole.

"She's only sixteen," her father had said to her mother back then. "Dammit, my daughter will not make a fool of herself, parading around with a *local* boy." He had not said "*Mexican* boy," though Marissa heard it all the same.

What had her mother said? Why had she not defended them? Marissa stared at the harbour, and for a moment, heard the echo of her mother reminding her to go to bed, to turn out the lights, to go to sleep. It's too late, she thought. Then she remembered that it didn't matter anymore. She could go to bed when she pleased, and get up at whatever hour she wanted, without anticipating the knock, knock, knock in early morning, her mother's voice urging her up, as if she were afraid that Marissa would remain in bed for a lifetime.

She stared out, imagining a new life for herself. In summer, hordes of tourists and picnickers would populate the beach beyond the road that dissected her yard from the ocean. They would barbeque on the grass, eat under the shade of pines, play volleyball on sand, race kites across the sky. There would be laughter and cheering and seagull squawks; the air would taste of salt and echo people's joy. People she could befriend, now that her mother was gone. She felt guilty instantly, thinking this, recalling those painful years when her mother had nursed her back to health, before her father died. It's all my fault, she thought. Her mother being on that bus. If only, she'd gone with her, if only … Headlights bored through the monotony of night. She lay down, turned out the lights, and in the darkness, a slow *drip…drip…drip…* began. She tried to imagine what it could be: a downspout near her window; a hose dripping into a bucket; perhaps the people next door had bought a rain barrel. But the sky was clear. She closed her eyes and counted backwards from 100, in threes. The drips fell into her dreams. They became the metronome beats of her childhood afternoons spent practising Liszt's *Hungarian Rhapsody*; the high-heel clicks of her mother's pacing overhead; the rhythmic splash of oars against black water. They became *drizzle, dew, mist, flurry, hail, sleet, snow, rain, tears.*

In the morning, she dialled the faded phone number tucked under the fridge magnet, and within the hour, a surly plumber arrived. He found no evidence of leaking pipes in the walls, nor faulty faucets, nor dripping sounds, and she felt a fool.

o o o

Later, after dinner at Curry Walla, Vivian and Freda wandered to the Temple Club — a double-decker hot spot they'd read about online, with an *apsara* floorshow upstairs, and cocktails, dancing, and snooker tables downstairs. They, too, were hot and between boyfriends.

Downstairs, the club teemed with tourists: young bronzed men in knee-length khaki shorts and baggy T-shirts; young women in jeans or skimpy skirts and halters, their dangly earrings glittering in candlelight. The air a-chatter, polyglot. Vivian and Freda stood at the bar, rum-and-Cokes in hand, dodging arms and legs on the dance floor. Vivian felt warm and slightly buzzing.

Freda's elbow prodded her side. "Over there," she whispered.

Vivian followed Freda's nod into the pool room, where two young men hovered, watching others play. They were tanned and blond with straight white teeth — probably German or Scandinavian, Vivian thought.

"I'm going to signal them over." Freda's eyes lowered. "Are you okay with that?"

Vivian shrugged, and sipped her drink.

Lukas, Steffen. Tall and lean. Austrian and German. The men stood near them, spieling a quick biography. They'd been here three days. "Canadian," Vivian and Freda said. "Four days." The sound system obliterated all efforts at talk. Vivian did not mind one bit. She didn't have the energy to ask or answer twenty questions. She didn't really want to know Steffen or Lukas. She only wanted to be alive, here in this place, tonight, without complications. Lukas asked her to dance, and she let him lead her onto the dance floor; immersed herself in the music's seductive rhythms, heartbeats, palpitations. She closed her eyes and conjured notes into the crannies of her brain, a swirling cacophony of overtones to exorcise thoughts. Steffen and Freda moved to a table, heads close together, speaking into each other's ears. Now and then, they sent rum-and-Cokes to the dance floor, which Vivian and Lukas downed, until the bass thrashed a headache into Vivian's brain. She pulled Lukas to one side.

"I need some fresh air," she said, searching in her purse for a Tylenol.

"I'll come too," Lukas said. "Too smoky."

Freda looked up. "Let's all get out of here," she said, running a hand through her long black hair, so that it shimmered and cascaded back down, water over stones. She followed Vivian and Lukas outside. "Let's do something fun."

"Like what?" Steffen asked when they were all standing in the street. He wore new white tennis shoes, their Nike swoosh flashing in the fluorescent street lights.

A few blocks up, the glow from the night market. A small boy darted across the street from one darkness to another, a baby strapped across his back. Dust rose from a passing taxi.

"I don't know…something frightening, something exciting." Freda was heady, almost jumping out of her Prada peep-toes.

"I've got a headache," Vivian said, but no one paid her any attention.

A near-full moon hung in the sky. Up the street, hand-painted signs of bars and restaurants competed for space at the edges of the unpaved road. A tuk-tuk pulled up, and Vivian recognized Mr. San straddling his meticulously clean moto, his helmet and black leather jacket incongruent with his fine features and melancholy eyes. Before she knew it, she bowed and pressed her hands together at chest level, as if she were praying. Mr. San nodded slightly, but did not return the Cambodian greeting.

"To Angkor Wat!" Lukas commanded, slapping the leather seat, as if it were a horse. Vivian cringed at the tone of his voice.

Mr. San removed his helmet and placed it behind him. "It is closed," he said. "I take you tomorrow at dawn."

"We want to go now," Lukas said. "We want to see something scary."

"Wats are sacred," Mr. San said. He stared defiantly at Lukas, hands on his knees. Sensitive, Vivian thought, with long fingers. A piano player's hands.

"What about all those demons guarding the gates?" Freda asked. "They must be guarding against something." She giggled and slipped her arm around Steffen. He grinned down at her, his head like that of a spiky blond porcupine.

Mr. San stared at them, unsmiling, inscrutable. In the open V of his shirt, tattooed letters — a *yantra*, Vivian thought, to ward off evil or bullets or grenades. She wondered if he were a soldier, or had been in his youth. *The bones cry out...* Goose bumps rose on her arms. Mr. San touched his heart.

"Come on, old man," Lukas said. "We want to see ghosts." He widened his eyes and spread out his arms in mock ghostly gestures.

"All country is filled with ghosts," Mr. San said quietly.

"Well, let's go see some then," Steffen said, helping Freda into the tuk-tuk, a friendly hand on her ass.

Mr. San scowled and turned away.

"I'm sorry," Vivian said as she climbed up. "We're a little drunk." They were being disrespectful, she thought, in a country where people practised sorcery and witchcraft, where people worshipped and feared a multitude of spirits and ghosts.

Mr. San did not respond. He donned his helmet, flicked on the motorbike and surged down the street.

The two couples sat across from each other: Vivian and Lukas gazed forward, watched the headlight cut a swath through the dark; Freda and Steffen faced a shifting shadowed past, eyes closed, locked in a kiss.

Vivian could feel Mr. San's disapproval, and see it in the sombre face and large pale eyes staring at her from the rear-view mirror.

"I know a nice dark place," Steffen said. His hand roved up Freda's skirt.

Vivian sat up straighter and slipped her arms into the sleeves of her hoody. The stone settled against her stomach. As Mr. San picked up speed, a cool wind rose. Lukas slid closer until his thigh was pressed against Vivian's, and she had nowhere to go. She shifted her weight to her outside leg, all the while trying not to stare at Freda and Steffen who sat across from her, tongues in each other's mouths, hands and fingers exploring each other's bodies.

"Freda," she said, and her friend opened her eyes.

Vivian tried to motion with her eyebrows, and with her own eyes. They'd only just met these men, for god's sake. She wished she had returned to the hotel.

"Lighten up," Freda said, winking at her. "You only live once." She closed her eyes, and sank back into Steffen.

"Come on," Vivian said. "You're not alone here."

Lukas casually extended his arm along the back of the seat, like a teenager in a movie theatre. Vivian felt his fingers on her shoulder, pulling her closer.

"Let them be," Lukas whispered. "They're having a good time." His breath was hot in her ear. She shivered, out of misplaced pleasure, arousal, but also out of discomfort for feeling this. She closed her eyes. Lukas mistook this as an amorous sign, and slid his hand around her waist, drawing her tight to him, his lips in her hair.

She made herself remain immobile, unsure what she wanted or felt. How was it that some things were so black and white when she thought about them, yet enveloped her in shades of grey when she was inside them? She glanced at Lukas, at his high delicate cheekbones, his blond curls, his green smiling eyes, his lips full and inviting. Then she saw the tuk-tuk driver's eyes in the rear-view mirror.

"Bring on the ghosts!" Lukas shouted into the darkness. Vivian shied from him, turned away, and stared at the black night, at the black jungle hurtling past them. A strange hum circled in her head. She thought she heard wailing, the thud of stones against flesh.

"What's the matter?" Lukas said. "Are you okay?" And she was brought back to herself in the tuk-tuk, with Freda and two strange men.

"I want to go back to the hotel," she said.

Freda looked up, as did Steffen, who yelled above the motor, "How much longer?"

Mr. San made a forward motion with his arm, to indicate nearby.

"Where are you taking us?" Freda said, giggling. "Is it scary?"

Mr. San's eyes were hard, hollow. Vivian felt them boring through her, judging her. He nodded. She wanted to shake her head, to say…to say what? That she was better than this? Different? *It's what you do that counts*, she told herself. Marissa's words the last time she phoned. Why hadn't Marissa returned her calls? She looked away. Mr. San soon turned left onto a less travelled road. The fat moon was high in the sky and shone a wide slash onto palm fronds. The tuk-tuk followed its own beam along the narrow road. They were utterly alone. For a moment, Vivian wondered if the men had conspired with this driver, if she and Freda were unsafe. She thought about all the things she'd never do back home. She'd certainly not get into a car with two strangers and head out into the jungle. She turned to look at Lukas, but the darkness was too thick, so she looked up instead at an aggregate of stars, stepping stones across time, across now and tomorrow and yesterday.

The tuk-tuk pulled to the side of the road and stopped abruptly. Mr. San turned off the motor, and they were hemmed in darkness. He pointed into what looked like a field, intermittent trees silhouetted in moonlight. To one side, three bamboo huts beside a mountain of trash. "Get out now," he said, his voice tight.

The four of them obeyed, although suddenly they were not laughing.

"What's this?" Lukas said. "Where have you brought us?"

Vivian stared into the field, her eyes growing accustomed to the dark. She could see pebbles, white stones protruding from the soil.

"This really is creepy," Freda said in a hushed voice. "Let's get out of here."

Mr. San stood at the side of the road, "There are your ghosts!" he said. "Go. Now," he pointed once more, his voice charged.

Vivian followed the command of his voice, stepped into the opening between two trees, and stood squinting at the dotted field.

"What kind of joke is this, old man?" Steffen said.

Mr. San came around and stood inches from Steffen. "This country," he said, "is graveyard. That field is wet with blood. That earth is full of bones. Go. Go and find your ghosts. They are everywhere." He turned, got on the motorbike and drove up the road, away from town.

"Great," Lukas said. "Some madman leaves us out in the middle of nowhere." He stamped his foot. "*Scheiße!*"

"Did anyone get his tuk-tuk number? We ought to report him," Steffen said.

"Who does he think he is?" Freda said.

Up the road, a few feet away, rose a small pagoda with steps leading up its four sides. The three of them walked over and sat on the bottom steps of the side facing the road. "I'm sure he'll be back to get us," Freda said. "He's probably trying to creep us out. We said we wanted to be scared. Let's sit tight and wait."

Vivian stayed behind, stood perfectly still, listening to the hum and wail inside her head. She could almost make out words. She bent her head toward the sound of... clicking, crickets... the din of bells ringing, quarter tones apart, a discordant sound building to unison, like a giant orchestra tuning up. And then a bass drum, beating — or was it her headache pounding — until she thought she heard gunshots, over and over and over. "He's right," she said finally, and they all turned to her. "There are ghosts everywhere. I can hear them."

"Vivian!" Freda yelled. "Don't *you* start acting crazy like your sister!"

"My sister is not crazy!" she said, thinking *she is*, thinking *there's something wrong with her*, thinking *I should have done something, should have, should have.* She crouched towards Freda, raised her arms and let out a shriek that sent Freda, Lukas and Steffen all scurrying up the steps. Then she followed them up slowly, until their backs were up against a plate-glass wall. "There are your ghosts," she said, pointing, and they turned.

Behind the glass, hundreds of skulls stared out of empty eyes. Freda screamed, and scrambled down the steps, Steffen and Lukas right behind her. They ran down the road a ways. Vivian watched them, tried to imagine Freda pelting her with stones, the impossible, only a stairway down.

"Don't be freaky!" Freda called out. "This is not funny."

Steffen took a card out of his wallet, and opened his cellphone. "I'll call us another tuk-tuk," he said. "That guy's a maniac." They continued down the road, the sound of their voices growing fainter.

o o o

Since her mother's death, no one had come to the house to offer condolences, and as long as Marissa did not go upstairs into her mother's room, she could pretend her mother was still alive, lying in bed, watching TV, writing letters to City Hall about noisy, inconsiderate neighbours.

She cleaned out the kitchen, threw away old boxes of crackers, cornstarch and Aunt Jemima pancake mix. Cans and bottled goods went into boxes for the food bank. Once she began, she could not stop. She filled large garbage bags with the contents of the fridge, the cupboards, the pantry, and set them outside. When the kitchen was completely empty, she went to Home Depot and bought two brushes, two rollers and one large can of paint, the colour of which reminded her of Mexico: music and sand and the tangerine walls of the outdoor restaurant where she and the boy rendezvoused. She went upstairs to her room and found an old CD she had bought from a busker at the airport and slipped it into the player. A haunting saxophone spiralled into the room. Such a lonely sound, she thought, propelled into that other time, the two of them standing in the shadow of a dusty palm whose leaves were projected in skeletal patterns over the boy, the spine of a fish. His head bent towards her, his eyes intent on hers. "Promise me," he'd said, his hands on her shoulders. "Together forever. Promise." And she had, although a small fear had left her breathless.

She felt suddenly exhausted — up all day, hadn't eaten since noon, and now the windows were black maws around her. *Drip… drip… drip.* She turned her head this way and that. How could she have lived here all these years, and never noticed it before? She flicked out the light and stood in darkness, waiting. But she only heard the saxophone melody, wailing like a siren around her. She crept upstairs and lay in bed; fumbled for the phone and dialled Vivian in Toronto. She told her answering machine about the drips, the water, begged Vivian to come home, though Vivian had never lived in this home.

Some nights, the drips became the ocean lapping in benign ripples on sand, then suddenly rising in gigantic breakers that smashed to shore. Those nights, when water broke through the roof, and walls, she awakened in a pool of sweat.

She'd been home a week already, and still had not entered her mother's bedroom. The rest of the house she'd slowly emptied and bagged. Outside, dozens of large plastic sacks leaned against the garage, awaiting pickup. She'd emptied drawers and cupboards, closets and bureaus. With each removal, she felt lighter and more detached, as if her memories, too, were twist-tied into tightly packed bags. In her room, in a box high up on a shelf, she found the snorkel, mask and flippers her father had bought her after their return from Mexico that disastrous Christmas. What did he think? That she would magically don them and…and what? She had never used them. She took them out of the box, tossed them into a plastic bag, and set it outside. She left the rest of her room untouched, as well as her mother's room, the room she still could not bring herself to enter.

For a couple of days now, she had been walking the beach for hours, beginning at dusk and staying on until dark, trying to re-imagine herself in a different life. *Try taking care of yourself,* Vivian's voice echoed in her ears. She had become so accustomed to listening to her mother, to silently following her instructions, that now she felt adrift, on the edge of something both exhilarating and strange. What would she do? She sat on a bleached log and stared across the water at the downtown cityscape in the distance, skyscrapers rising like obelisks in the mist. She would get her part-time job back at the bookstore, she thought. She loved books, the interior lives of characters she could relate to, the adventures of people who could not harm her. She would join a health club, buy a second-hand bike, cycle to work on dry days, and ride the Skytrain on rainy wet ones. She would get a dog and walk along the beach, throw balls and Frisbees, and chat with other dog owners. She would make friends now that her mother was gone.

On that fateful holiday in Mexico, she and the boy had walked hand-in-hand on the beach, following the curve of the bay, beyond the last house. The moon was low on the horizon, and the surf up and angry, like a god disturbed. Waves advanced in dark, silent lines, building in height as they reached the shore. The boy pulled her to the edge of the sand, where all the water peaked, curled, then slapped down hard in triumphant explosions. She tried to move back, but the boy held her in the frothy water that licked up the beach, and receded, dragging them in its undertow.

He laughed at her fear, a test, she thought. She would do anything for him.

When they had reached the halfway point around the bay, he led her up the shore to a dilapidated building that stood alone, its back to the swamp where she'd heard Morelet's crocodiles roamed. She had seen this structure in the daytime, the graffitied concrete, the iron grate in front of the opening, rebar protruding from the walls at odd angles; had been told it was built as a seafood restaurant but never completed. The boy unlocked the iron grate and pulled her inside, onto the blanket he had prepared for them. They had undressed hurriedly in that darkness — she, timid, this being her first time — and made feverish love, and he had asked her to marry him, his voice rising above the pull and push of riptides.

# SOLITUDES

Vivian sat in the dark on the top step of the small pagoda and stared into the skulls. Of course she knew about Pol Pot, about the killing fields. Between 1975 and 1978, almost two million people starved, tortured, murdered. She'd read that Kang Kek lew, one of the leaders of the Khmer Rouge who was in charge of the notorious S-21 prison, had been indicted in 2007, and in custody for the past two years, pending his trial in a few months by an international tribunal. Thirty-one years after the fact. It seemed incredible that no one had been charged earlier, that no one had avenged the dead. She lay down on the top step, reached into her pocket, and put the visionary stone in her mouth. It was supposed to give her clarity, to give her, in dreams, the answer to a question. Back home, Vivian's jar of coloured stones guarded against various real or imagined illnesses — smoky quartz for inertia; carnelian for toxicity; tiger eye for indigestion; rhodonite for hypertension; turquoise for sore throat; amethyst for nightmares; lapis for anxiety; pyrite for migraines … *Where are you, Marissa?* she asked, and found herself in the middle of the field, surrounded by vertebrae, sternums, ribs, femurs, tibias, fibulas protruding from the earth — hundreds, thousands of bones, as if they had suddenly rustled to the surface of the field.

A rattling began from the pagoda; the skulls battered the glass, angry ghosts, decapitated, yearning for release. Above the field, the sky was a cumulus of faces, black-and-white, burning in and out of focus. Men, women, children, with black haunted eyes. They wanted something from her. But what? She pushed them away, but there were more and more and more, until they became a blur of black and white, bones and earth.

"My father is one of those." Mr. San's voice rose out of the darkness.

Vivian sat up and looked around her. She was still on the top step, beside the mound of skulls. She could not see Mr. San or the tuk-tuk. Instead of fear, she felt immensely tired. How could she possibly understand anything, the damage? "I'm sorry," she said, and put her head down on her knees.

"I don't know which one," he said.

"I heard they charged Nuon Chea with genocide," she said. "You'll finally have justice."

"Justice?" he asked. "Will they bring back the dead?"

"Maybe they'll ask forgiveness," Vivian said.

"How can they ask forgiveness when they don't admit to be wrong?"

"I think my sister is dead," Vivian said. "And it's my fault."

They both sat, silent and still until an owl screeched in a swoop of wings. "They tell us to forget," he said. "But it's like you step in a puddle and get your pants wet. And thirty years later, they have not dried."

The air felt thick and melancholy. "And you?" Vivian said. "How did you escape your father's fate?"

He didn't answer for a while, and Vivian waited, her heart heavy. Presently, he said, "I was afraid to die." He stepped out of the shadows and sat on the bottom step, looking away from her. "If we kill of our own free will," he said, "that's evil. But if we are ordered to…"

"What are you saying?" Vivian said.

"I was afraid," he said.

o o o

On the beach now, in Vancouver, a red sun, low on the horizon was reflected in the multiple windows of the downtown skyscrapers, creating a burning cathedral.

The splash startled her. She turned. A man rose slowly out of the waves, a black masked figure, trails of seaweed on his back. Water *dripped, splashed, trilled, spouted, bled, wept, trickled* onto sand. She drew in her breath. It couldn't be. Her heart beat frantic rhythms in her chest. She got up and raced home, locked the doors, closed all the windows and secured them. Then, she went up to her bedroom, and looked out. In the twilight, she could just discern the man on the sand. He had shed the top half of his wetsuit, so that it hung like a second skin around his waist. Behind him, partly in water, was a windsurfer, its blue sail floating on the water's surface. She sighed, let out a small laugh. She was being ridiculous. She unlatched the windows and breathed in.

Downstairs a few moments later, when she opened the door, he stood, dripping, on the wooden porch, his rubber mask dangling around his neck. "I couldn't help noticing," he said. He shifted foot to foot, as if trying to keep warm in the blue Teva water sandals, his skin chafed red in the January air. "Back there...."

She stared at him, listening to the water drip off his wetsuit into the depressions in the porch where water clustered, forming a glass harmonica of chromatic runs, pentatonic scales, minor modes, a dissonance —

"I frightened you," he said. "I'm sorry."

She took a deep breath, back to herself. "No, no, it was nothing..." And when he continued to stare at her, she added, "An error, that's all... I mistook you for someone..." She ran a hand through her hair, aware she must look dishevelled.

He smiled and stamped his feet. A rainbow of water sprayed out of his hair, which was black and sleek as an eel. "Are you all right?"

She nodded, uncertain. She must have appeared crazy back there. She rubbed her forehead, dredging up calming techniques. "Think of desert islands and bright sunny beaches," her mother used to say, as if these would calm her. But Marissa had no sense of a meditative space where she was happy. Instead she placed tiny green tablets under her tongue, and counted until the knots in her stomach and chest dissolved.

"I heard your mother died," he said.

She frowned. *How did he know? Why was he here?* Should she close the door and throw the latch? Her hand slid around the door knob.

"I'm sorry." His eyes were black and avoided hers.

"Yes, no, thank you. An accident." She flicked on the porch light overhead, and he was silhouetted against a violet sky. The street was deserted.

"Well. You're sure you're okay?" His head now craned around hers, his eyes stared past her, into the living room.

*What was he seeing? What was he looking for?* "My father should be here at any moment," she lied, trying to keep her voice from trembling. Beyond him on the porch lay bags and bags of the house interior, Marissa's old life cinched into black plastic. Safe.

"It's awfully cold out here," he said, his voice confidential. "My windsurfer's broken, and my car's way off at Third Beach."

"I'm sorry," she said, and began closing the door, when his foot stepped in.

"Would you mind if I used your phone to call a friend to come and get me?" He smiled.

Too late, she saw her mistake. She had been right to run. His eyes, the hue of his hands. She couldn't tell whether he was alive or dead; whether she was alive or dead, then or now, his voice urging her back, her whole being wanting to surrender. "You must go," she whispered. "Please." Then she was crying against his chest, his arms around her, his words soothing, "There. There." Slowly, he pushed the door open and walked her inside, backwards, as if they were dancing, until he sat her gently on the couch. She was sobbing loudly now, and shivering, her shirt damp. She covered her face with her hands, and dropped her head onto her knees. She was utterly alone.

o o o

Late morning, Vivian left Freda asleep in the hotel and tiptoed out like a regretful lover, holding the door until it clicked shut. She walked to the end of the hall, and the further she was from the door, the quicker and lighter her steps became, until she reached the circular staircase, and now she skipped down as though relieved of a great weight. She slipped her hand into her pocket and fingered the smooth face of the moonstone. The previous night swung, turbulent, in her thoughts. She hoped she would not see Lukas or Steffen, or Mr. San, whose confession had precipitated this unspooling. How could victims and perpetrators live side-by-side, intrinsically linked, stupefied and cruel? What did she know about this kind of evil? She, who could not help her own sister.

Up the main road, past the manicured gardens of restored colonial hotels, away from the throng of buses and taxis, she drifted until there were no more guest houses, no western restaurants, no bars. Slowly, the paved road disintegrated into a gravel road, and she found herself in the midst of dusty shanty huts with woven walls, and open markets whose stands were bloody with the carcasses of animals. Women squatted on the ground, shelling nuts, their ragged children scattered around them. The men stared out of haunted eyes — were they all damaged then? How to escape one's own dark history?

o   o   o

Marissa next awakened in her mother's bed, and sat up, alarmed. She was fully dressed, and the clock on the nightstand read 7:06 p.m. Had she been sleeping an hour or a full day? The open shutters cast indigo bars onto her skin. The first thing she saw was the book she had given the boy. *Mythology: Timeless Tales of Gods and Heroes.* Her chest ached with longing, knowing how the boy had dreamt of going to university, although his parents disapproved and wanted him to work in his father's blacksmith shop. *Are your own kind not good enough?* they'd said. She opened the book, its yellowed pages, and there, on page 39, marking *The Underworld*, was the coin. In the margins of the page, the words: *Safe Passage.* She shrank from it. How did it get there? She turned quickly, as if expecting...whom? But there was no one. Her mother's bed rumpled, the sinister shutters half-open, her purple suitcase by the door, as though she had stepped out and would return at any moment. On the dresser the coin beckoned, the ocean roaring in her ears. *I'm not a very good swimmer,* she'd told the boy. Who could have known? Who could have put it there? She felt her spine tingle, pulled her sweater closer. They had talked about death, of course, in the way teenagers are drawn to the dark, fascinated by myth and legend. The coin, the boy had told her, was to pay the ferryman, Charon, for passage across the rivers Styx and Acheron, which divided the world of the living from that of the dead. If one did not pay the fee, he was destined to wander the shores for 100 years.

Waves thundered in, combined with outgoing ones, doubled in size, leapt in the air, curled and furled in madness. Her father had dragged her out of that building, half-dressed, even as she pleaded with him. In Mexico, girls married at sixteen, she'd said. *I love him.* But her father had dragged her back to the Villas Camino del Mar. Only later, when everyone was sleeping, had she been able to sneak out, paying a small bribe to the night watchman, who nodded towards the shadows where the black-haired boy awaited.

They had returned to the rundown building and set fire to it, swearing to be together always. Watched the eruption of flames, smoke stinging their eyes. Then, he had urged her into his small boat though she was terrified of water, of the tide surging around them, the undertow. She once almost drowned as a child, but she had followed him, nonetheless, trembling in surrender.

"Don't be afraid," the boy had said, rowing them little by little away from the shore, waves rising around them. She shivered in the darkness, hands clasped tightly to the boat's sides, watching the moon's sliver of light undulate on water. She wondered if her parents would notice her absence. She felt adrift, on the edge of something both liberating and discomforting.

She couldn't see the expression on his face, only the dark silhouette of his taut body against the air. When they were sufficiently away from the lights and the shore, when the ocean rose around them, lapping against the sides of the boat, he had locked in the oars and thrown an anchor overboard. Then he'd moved to the bottom of the boat, and pulled her to him.

"We're meant for this."

She'd felt alarmed suddenly, as if she had allowed herself to step beyond the boundaries of her own common sense, of her own fears. She wondered if her parents were missing her yet. From this angle inside the boat, the lights of the village and the burning building were a distant beacon in the night sky. She could only feel the heat of him beside her. His hand reached for hers, and placed a coin in it.

"What's this?"

"For passage," he said. "Put it under your tongue."

"I want to go back," she said. "My parents are worried."

But he held her to him, fingers digging into her forearm. She trembled, shook her head.

"Keep your promise." His voice was harsh, and his fingers burned around her wrist. "It's time." He began to stand up, and the boat swayed.

"We can wait until I turn eighteen," she said, her voice rising. "I'll come back. No one will stop us then." She pushed against him, frightened by his intensity, the coin pressed into her fist. What had she done? She was sweating, her whole body damp, despite the cold breeze. His hand tightened around her wrist.

"You *know* this is the only way we can be together," he said, "forever." He slipped the coin into his mouth, and pulled her over the edge into the water.

At first, she'd thrashed horribly, fought against the boy whose hands struggled to keep her against him, before a large wave separated them, and she was pulled under, dragged by the weight of water. When she surfaced, gasping, she could not see or hear him above the sound of the ocean. She had managed, by not panicking, to slowly progress to shore by floating on her back, doing breaststrokes, backstrokes, crawls, until she felt the sandy bottom against her legs.

But the boy was never found.

On the dresser, the coin was a stark reminder of their childish pact, the little vow buried at sea.

A slow dripping began again. She palmed the coin and followed the sounds out of her mother's bedroom, down the stairs, to the gush of *freshet, rivulet, current, tide, torrent, milk sweat, urine, blood.*

She ran across the road amid the blare of car honks and the screech of brakes until she saw him. He was at the edge of the bay, dripping, only half-submerged. He wore goggles and she couldn't see his face. *I'm sorry, I'm sorry, I'm so sorry*, she said. She thought about her mother, wandering the shores for 100 years.

He opened his arms.

She stopped, uncertain, the water slowly rising, her feet digging into the sand, but he reached out and held her wrist.

"I can't swim well." Her jeans now clung to her thighs, and her voice shook, but she followed him into the water.

The cold numbed her immediately. She kicked her feet and slid silently among the waves. Ahead, a chiaroscuro summoned. She sliced through water, head down, teeth tight, the smooth glide of waves on her back, hypnotized by the black tendrils enticing her further and further out. She felt no longer like herself.

When she looked up, the sea billowed around her. She was alone, in the middle of the harbour, amid thundering waves, the Point Grey shore now too far to reach. Here and there, the massive shapes of ocean liners mocked her with festive fairy lights.

She called out to them, trying to keep herself from panicking. "Please, someone, help me!" She fought to keep her head above the crests, fought against the weight of water in her lungs. Then his liquid arms grasped her, *forever, forever,* and she sank against the deep, gasping, sobbing in gratitude, swimming within that tight embrace farther and farther out.

o o o

Vivian walked and walked, until in late afternoon, she ducked into an internet café nestled between a palm and an oleander, and emailed Marissa. Phoned once again, but this time, got an out-of-service message. She wondered if Marissa kept her phone number folded in her wallet. She Googled Vancouver hospitals and called each one, asking if her sister had been admitted. An hour later, when she emerged from the internet café, the man was sitting by the door, as if he had been expecting her. He wore the same faded crimson shirt and jeans, but from his feet dangled bamboo flip-flops. She wondered suddenly what he might have seen or done as a child. How easy it would be to fall into suspicion, she thought. Neighbours fearing neighbours.

She recoiled from his outstretched hand. "Help," he said.

Did he recognize her? She scrounged in her purse for a wrinkled bill and held it out.

He shook his head, his eyes looking at hers, beyond hers, as if focused at a point inside her.

What did he want? She smiled, but he continued to stare at her, his head lolling from side to side. She walked around him, stepped off the sidewalk and crossed the street. She needed to clear her head, to make some decision about Marissa. She'd fly to Vancouver and find her a facility. Or she could bring her back to Toronto to live with her. Every time she turned, the man was skulking behind her. "Go away," she'd say, motioning him with her hands.

He'd stop.

However, a block up when she turned again, he'd be following. What did he want? She felt her stomach knot.

She hailed a tuk-tuk and felt better as soon as they drove out of the area, and back towards the Old Market and restaurants. "Drive around the temples," she said. She wanted to get away from the man, from pressing need. She pulled out her guidebook and flipped through it. Tomorrow she'd be flying home, and still she had not seen Ta Prohm, the temple that represented how the entire complex of Angkor Wat appeared when the French naturalist Henri Mouhot rediscovered it in 1861 while searching for butterflies and beetles. Whereas the other temples were in the process of or had been restored, Ta Prohm, abandoned for three centuries, was reclaimed by the jungle.

They arrived an hour before closing, when most buses were leaving the complex, the air blue with diesel fumes. The driver dropped her off at the west entrance gate. Ahead of her in the distance, the last straggler of a tour group turned a corner, and Vivian found herself alone. Had she seen a black plastic bag in his hand? Above her were four faces carved into a magnificent stone pavilion, their eyes immutable, all-seeing. The King's eyes. What had they witnessed through centuries? If only they could speak.

The sky had begun to cloud, bathing everything in a greyish hue. Vivian took off her hat and used it to dry her forehead. The tour group had vanished, or maybe it was hovering out of sight, behind the rust-coloured rubble that in the late afternoon light began to assume sinister shapes. Each massive block had a hole bored into it. A thousand years ago, men had carved those holes, passed rope through them, and then attached the ropes to elephants who dragged the stones from the Kulen hills, forty kilometres to the northeast of Siem Reap to their present locations. She tried to imagine elephants chained, plodding through the hot dusty terrain, through jungle foliage and flooded riverbeds, their heads bent, their long trunks swirling in the air.

The man ducked around the corner to the right — this time, she was sure it was him — his crimson shirt unmistakeable. Her heart fluttered against the cage of her ribs. She looked back at the entrance gate, but it was too far, too deserted, and anyhow, the driver was to pick her up at the east gate. She turned to the left, away from him.

A sound began, like continuous bells chiming, and as she walked, it swelled, until she realized it was cicadas in the enormous banyan tree whose roots clutched a temple wall, as if trying to detach it from the rest of the structure. As she approached, instead of roots, she saw white fingers elongated to claws, large monsters, parasites, gripping the temple balustrade, like demons come to challenge the faithful, toppling beliefs, toppling God, Buddha, Shiva, in a powerful show of strength.

The man appeared in a doorway in front of her.

Vivian waved him off. She hurried through a portal, teetered over a collapse of blocks, sharp stone edges digging into her sandals. Found herself in a crumbling courtyard, surrounded by the maws of porticoes askewed by the talons of a sacred fig.

The man followed.

Vivian scrambled across and passed through three small temples, delving deeper and deeper into a maze. At every turn, she saw only more rubble, more temples. The man's breath echoed behind her. She stopped and pointed at him sternly. "Go away," she said again. "Go, go."

The man paused: "*Niak teuv naa?*"

She climbed up a wooden stairway to her right and stopped at a terrace. The sun was dropping quickly, eclipsed by thick clouds. All around, brown and sandstone blocks were piled high, as if to form an insurmountable impediment, greyish-green with lichen and shadow. She hurried along a cloistered walkway until it ended abruptly in another courtyard, bounded by walls with blind doors and square piers filled with dancing *apsaras*. Her heart was beating hard in her chest. She took deep breaths to calm herself, then began to scramble across the mountain of ruins.

"Why are you running?" Marissa said, and Vivian turned, startled.

Her sister stood across from her, leaning against a blind door. She held out her hand. "Why didn't you help me?" she said.

Vivian closed her eyes. "Go away," she said, but her voice lacked conviction. She fingered the stone in her pocket. *Concentrate on something positive*, she told herself, willing a blank screen in the front of her mind. Her apartment back home. But the *besach* pulled at the corners of her screen, skeletal hands ripping, ripping open a dark night, water rising, a shipwreck in the harbour. Her heart pounded in her ears. She stifled a call for help, though there was no one. Made herself count slowly to ten. When she opened her eyes, the man stood where Marissa had been, indistinguishable from the bilious stones. He advanced toward her, emboldened by their proximity.

"*Please.* I can't give you anything. Go away," Vivian said, louder now, her voice hysterical.

The shadow scurried across a dark row of pillars.

"Go away, I'm warning you," Vivian said, tears springing in her eyes. She leaned down and picked up a stone.

# PERMANENT TOURISTS

o o o

*Sometimes, only one person is missing,*
*and the whole world seems depopulated.*

—Alphonse de Lamartine

### ELLEN

The old mirror set in a wooden frame buckles and waves Ellen's face as she applies mascara. She both recognizes herself and doesn't, her features distorted with every move. If she were living in ancient times, she might interpret this as an omen of her fate. A distorted life. She shakes off the thought. She ought to throw out the old mirror, smash it into a million pieces just to prove those stupid superstitions wrong.

To the right of the counter, a strange object grows and shrinks across the surface according to her head movement. She frowns, sets down the mascara brush, and picks up a small glass jar with a pink lid, face cream. How did that get there? *Mika*, she thinks. But it's impossible. Ellen opens drawers, looks under the sink, peruses the medicine cabinet, but nothing looks out of place. She takes a deep breath and tells herself to calm down.

She finishes applying makeup, combs her hair in an updo, aware of the jar at the corner of the counter. She doesn't want it there. She touches it again, to make sure it's something solid, real, then picks it up and takes it to the guest bathroom. She pauses at the door of the guest bedroom, almost afraid to look inside. However, when she pushes open the door, she sees only the pale blue bedspread and matching pillow shams. She lets out a long breath.

"Mika?" she says to the empty room, but no one replies.

She goes into the kitchen, brews coffee, then sits at the counter. There's no reason to put on makeup or comb her hair, or get dressed for that matter, other than to make herself feel that she's "participating in life," as her daughter Joyce is always encouraging her to do. She hasn't been out of the house in five years.

She calls Joyce and waits through eight rings. "Have you heard from your sister?" she asks, when her daughter's sleepy voice finally answers.

"Mom," Joyce says after a long pause.

"I found something in my bathroom," Ellen says. "Maybe she's back."

"Mom," Joyce says again. "Where are you?"

"In the kitchen." Ellen's voice lowers to a whisper. "It's not what you think."

"Take a deep breath," Joyce says. "Calm down. I'll get dressed and come by."

Ellen hangs up and sighs. She goes back to the kitchen, opens the cutlery drawer, lifts the tray, and pulls out an Amber Alert poster. She stares at Mika's twelve-year-old face. She'd be twenty-two now.

A half hour later, Joyce sits across from her at the kitchen table, her face anxious, her eyes questioning.

"Other children have been found," Ellen says. "There was the one just last month, who was kept captive for ten years, then was found." Ellen scours the internet for stories of abducted children who have been rescued. Jaycee Dugard was eleven when she was taken, only a year younger than Mika, and she was found after eighteen years. And that Austrian girl who was kept locked in a basement for twenty-four years. She was found. Or Elizabeth

Smart or Steven Stayner, or Shawn Hornbeck or Abby Drover. They were all found years and years after their kidnapping.

"The police have done…are doing all they can," Joyce says.

"No, they're not. Or they would have found her." Even as she says this, however, Ellen knows this is not true. How were they to find a child who disappeared without a trace?

For a long time, the police had investigated them all: husband, uncles, grandparents, friends. Everyone was suspect. The child had vanished so easily that she must have gone with someone familiar, someone no one identified as a stranger. She had simply not been there when Ellen arrived to pick her up.

Ellen does not believe the police. This is not the first time Mika has left her imprint in the house. A couple of months ago, Ellen discovered the cutlery drawer rearranged, and a strange-looking honey spoon added. Another time, she found two pairs of winter boots and a jacket in the hall closet, though it was summer. On yet another occasion, she was sure the photos on the mantelpiece had been switched around, and once, she found bedding folded on the couch, as if Mika had slept there. She called Joyce after each of these occurrences, but Joyce told her it was nothing, that she was imagining things, that she must have moved the items herself, fallen asleep in front of the TV. She must have forgotten, Joyce said. It was natural. Nothing to worry about. Ellen protested, of course, but in the end, she was cowed by Joyce's shrugs and frowns which implied she was making it all up, that she was losing her mind, that she only wanted attention, that she was making an unnecessary fuss.

Ten years. She knows everyone believes Mika is dead, died probably soon after she was taken. That's what all the statistics say: *the first forty-eight hours are crucial. The more time passes, the less likely to find the child alive.* They simply haven't found the remains. She knows the police aren't looking for a live Mika. They have only to wait until some hiker discovers a shallow grave deep in the woods somewhere.

"She's trying to contact us," Ellen tells Joyce now. "That's why she's been leaving me things."

"That makes no sense," Joyce says, reaching across the table to touch her hand. "If she wanted to contact us, she could just call."

"I meant…spiritually…from afar…" her voice trails off.

"Mom, you're talking nonsense. The evidence you're using is physical. Either you're moving things around and forgetting, or someone's breaking into your apartment."

"Never mind," Ellen says.

After Joyce leaves, Ellen paces through the apartment, looking for other clues.

What tortures her is that just before Mika disappeared, Ellen, who is/was a social worker, was doing a wellness check on a pair of twins in a foster home, after which she'd stopped for a quick coffee and a chat with a friend at Starbuck's, arriving at the school twenty minutes late. However, she'd been late before, and Mika had simply waited in one of the classrooms. Someone must have been watching the playground, must have seen the opportunity.

She plays and replays that last day, willing a different ending. What if she hadn't gone to that last appointment? What if she hadn't stopped for coffee? It's all my fault, she thinks, though she's never admitted this to anyone.

In the months that followed Mika's disappearance, she and her husband Jeff went to a marriage counsellor, fully aware that a lost or dead child places an unimaginable burden on a relationship. Ellen tried to continue to be a good mother to Joyce, who now tiptoed around the house, as if she were afraid that she'd remind her parents of their missing child. As the months and years passed, Joyce began to disappear for a day or two, and Ellen panicked and reported her missing to the police, who soon began to tell her that they considered Joyce a runaway, not a missing person. Ellen went back to work as soon as she could manage not to cry through interviews and house visits. Her supervisor warned her that she was being "too vigilant," too quick to judge people, to scrutinize their motives; she suggested counselling.

Ellen and Jeff carried on like this for five years, and when Joyce turned eighteen, they divorced, both exhausted from the effort of sustaining some semblance of a normal life. They split their savings and moved into separate apartments. Joyce disappeared more often, but now she was working for an agency organizing and leading budget tours across the world. Ellen quit her job and stopped going out.

"For God's sake, Mother!" Joyce kept saying, "You're only forty-nine. You're not dead. You should be getting out, meeting people."

But Ellen only shook her head.

Joyce brought her groceries, did her banking, paid her bills. "You need to go back to therapy," she often said.

Ellen's ex-husband was supportive — surely they still loved each other? — and deposited monthly cheques into her account.

And now this. Ellen is certain Mika is trying to contact her, despite what Joyce says. She sits in front of the TV and watches travel documentaries set around the globe.

From Amazon.ca, she receives near-daily packages of travel paraphernalia — the perfect carry-on, a luxury cosmetic case of tiny airplane-friendly plastic bottles, a yellow raincoat, a collapsible sunhat, a caftan in oranges and purples, a blue beach towel stamped with a black palm tree, sunscreen and mosquito repellent.

When she turns on the TV at night to watch *Waterfront Cities of the World*, or *Globe Trekker*, or *Travels at the Edge*, or Anthony Bourdain's *No Reservations*, or *Departures*, or *Parts Unknown*, she dons the appropriate clothes, as if she, too, were on an African safari, swimming in the Indian Ocean, trekking through the Himalayas, spelunking in a Slovenian cave.

Joyce calls from airports, using the free WiFi. "I'm in Vietnam," she says, "Cambodia, Laos, Thailand. I'm in France, Germany, Switzerland, Italy. I'm in South Africa, Tanzania, Zimbabwe, Botswana. I'm in…"

Ellen cherishes these calls and writes down the names of villages, towns and cities, monuments, art galleries and game reserves, national parks, campgrounds and hotels. Later, she searches the internet and YouTube videos, so the next time her daughter calls, she can say, "I was with you, my daughter. How beautiful it was!"

She closes her eyes, cinches her belt, her brain in transit.

o o o

*The reality is you will grieve forever.*
*You will not "get over" the loss of a loved one;*
*you will learn to live with it.*
*You will heal and you will rebuild yourself*
*around the loss you have suffered.*
*You will be whole again*
*but you will never be the same.*

—Elisabeth Kübler-Ross

## FERRIS

When he was in his twenties and studying geology, Ferris fancied himself an inventor, having invented a variety of objects — artificial stones made from sand, gravel, soil and wood ash; a fire extinguisher using chloride of magnesium; a gemstone polishing machine; a road surface made from pyrite — for which he had registered patents, though none of them had been bought. It seemed as soon as he invented something, someone else produced something like it, or more advanced, so that he was forever just a step behind. Then, an opportunity presented itself: a week-long Wellness Fair, featuring products to stimulate mind and body growth.

He invented, registered, and produced the prototype for a compact, heated simulated rock for massage. Rumour was that Cindy Crawford was coming to the Fair to scout for products to sponsor. Ferris decided his invention was perfect for her. He rented a booth at the Fair and for a week waited for Cindy Crawford, who never materialized. No one bought his invention. His letter to Crawford's manager detailing his simulated rock went unanswered.

His friends had turned this anecdote into a metaphor for what they called his "impossibility of motion."

Two decades later, Ferris lives in a downtown condo — a large studio on the eighteenth floor — glass walls like waterfalls flowing ceiling to hardwood, a Murphy bed concealed behind the fake bookcase — a studio for one. His geo-décor consists of stones of various shapes, sizes, hues, clustered on the floor, on his teak coffee table, to one side of the granite kitchen counter, haphazardly, as if the condo were the remains of an interior rock slide he can't be bothered to clear away.

It's not that he's particularly messy, but rather that he returns from his frequent trips with sacks of stones he deposits wherever he finds space. If he were to continue like this, he would soon be walled in.

His relationships accumulate, like his stones, one on top of the other, the most recent always on shiny display, while the others fade under the weight of disappointment.

He loves women in an abstract way: their energy, their scent, their laughter; dates each for a finite time, then moves on, because, he tells them, he is always travelling to a new mine, always in foreign countries to analyze stones and metals. He has no time for commitment. His condo is too small. And he flees before the tears and reproaches.

His latest, for example, is Tanja — thirty-three, a single mother of two — whom he has been dating on and off for the past two months. They text, have dinner now and then. Sleep together in her apartment, where his memories cannot intrude. What attracted Ferris to Tanja was her attentiveness, her easy demonstrative, affectionate ways, which have now become suffocating, as if she were slowly rising water.

"Why can't you get serious about her?" his friend Vincent says on one of their Thursday Happy Hours in a sports bar.

"It's not like that," Ferris says. He likes Tanja, and he likes being around her, though after a few hours he can't wait to get away. He's conflicted by his own inability to define his feelings, as if he were one of those pathetic TV Bachelors, trying to decide which of the desperate Bachelorettes he should marry.

Vincent raises his eyebrows. "You've been spending a lot of time together."

Ferris shifts in his chair. "Not really," he says.

They silently watch a golf game on TV for a while, both of them nursing a beer.

"Milly's been on my case for a holiday," Vincent says during the commercial, referring to his live-in girlfriend. "We could go somewhere warm. The four of us."

"I don't know …," Ferris says. "I'm about to leave town … Tanja might get the wrong idea …" He tries to imagine if he could spend entire days and nights with her.

A month later, the four of them are booked into a two-week stay in Long Beach, California.

Ferris does his best: he spends lazy afternoons playing cards with the others, drinks tall cool gin-and-tonics around the pool of their hotel in the daytime, plays volleyball on the vast beach, wanders bars in the evenings. The four of them get along splendidly. Ferris hardly spends any time alone with Tanja, which suits him very well.

They rent bikes and head off along the waterfront, passing rental shops for Jet Skis, kayaks, boats, and windsurf boards; park their bikes and wander among the platforms of vendors who, under market umbrellas, sell straw hats, guidebooks, bathing suits, cover-ups, pashminas in every colour of the rainbow. A young busker plays guitar and sings a repertoire of Beach Boys songs.

Milly holds up her phone to frame the four of them in a selfie. Ferris resists, moving away from them. He watches them laugh for the camera, imagining the posts on Facebook and Instagram. Look at me! these selfies will say. I'm having a good time. Selfies — a form of narcissism Ferris can neither condone nor understand. He grew up in a family that valued books and human interaction. His mother punctuated her opinions and ideas with literary references. When others spouted platitudes; his mother recited poems. Right now, in this situation, she would be quoting P.K. Page's "The Permanent Tourists" who wander the world: *with their empty eyes/ longing to be filled with monuments*. Well, nowadays, he thinks, no one wants to be filled with anything but their own reflections.

The four of them ride back to their hotel, a series of ocean-front cottages surrounded by lush gardens. Caged birds line the open lobby, and Ferris feels a momentary panic seeing them, so large and exotic, trapped in such small confined spaces. He wants to open the cage doors and release them. He feels a sudden longing to be back home. He shouldn't have come. He should have told Tanja that he didn't love her. Instead, he follows her to the reception desk, where they retrieve their room key, then sit on the veranda and watch surfers in the waves beyond.

"It's so good we are here," Tanja says, opening one of the vodka bottles they bought at the duty-free store. She pours three fingers into his glass and hands it to him.

"Thank you," he says, grateful for the drink. The liquid warms his throat and slowly dispels his restlessness.

*You're an alcoholic*, his wife said, the night of the terrible fight, the night he insisted on driving the car. *Don't kid yourself*. Ferris does not consider himself an alcoholic, despite her accusation. It's true that he has three of these drinks every night, maybe half a bottle, but he's never drunk. Alcoholics drink all day, he thinks, and don't hold down day jobs. Alcoholics abandon their families and drink themselves to death, like his father did.

Tanja reaches across and strokes his cheek, a gesture he finds irritating. "Oh," she says in a warm voice, "you are feeling better, no?"

He moves his head out of her reach. "Yes, yes, much better. It's the heat." In his head, he practises ways of telling her: *I really like you, but... You're a good friend, but... I enjoy being with you, but...*

Tanja smiles and sips her tall glass of soda water. He would prefer to hear her admonish him, tell him that he's ruining his health, that he's killing brain cells. Then he'd have something to push back against.

In the morning, they pile into the rented car Vincent arranged, and head to Terranea Cove Beach, to hike to and explore a large sea cave at low tide. Caves are Vincent's special interest. He spends a lot of time reading about them, fascinated, fantasizing about spending a year or two visiting nothing but caves across the country. Caves, Ferris thinks, are ambiguous, both protective and dangerous. In a cave, the blackness becomes one's own soul, the thin air an abandonment, the silence unstable, lawless, a whirl of chaos. Caves are wombs in the earth, places of worship, concealment, and isolation, portals to other worlds — the Underworld, the supernatural, one's inner self.

They park the car and set off down the path to the cave. Every step increases his apprehension. His guilt weighs him down. He must tell Tanja that it's hopeless between them. He must go home.

"Come on," Tanja says, excitedly, when they reach the beach. She has never been inside a cave. Vincent and Milly sprint ahead, while Ferris lags behind. They scramble on the rocky beach, wading around a point to get to the cave.

Years ago, before his wife's death, Ferris had routinely descended rope ladders in Mexican mines, double-decker cages in South Africa, even iron buckets in long-abandoned mines in Scotland. But now, any enclosed space recalls the swerve into the lake, water rising, his wife screaming, his breathlessness and panic. These days, he chooses jobs studying earth processes like earthquakes, floods and landslides, surveying land for development, investigating metals and minerals in open-pit mines, never underground.

"What if the tide comes in and we get stuck inside?" he says. Earlier this year, Japan was hit by a 9.0 magnitude earthquake that caused a massive tsunami. Ferris had watched the live footage and the replays of the devastating waves that churned everything in their path. In the videos, people, cars, trucks, boats, houses were all reduced to bouncing miniatures, as if made of balsa wood, easily smashing against each other. He eyes the Long Beach ocean now, anxious. And then not a month later, there was that terrible story of the diver stunt woman for the film *Sanctum*, who became disoriented and ran out of air while manoeuvring through eight kilometres of underwater passages in a cave in Australia. The recovery rescue dive itself was heart-stopping. He'd watched it live on TV. How did those divers keep from panicking? He imagines for a moment the four of them trapped inside this sea cave, water rising up. He imagines the fight for breath, feels the intake of his own.

"The tide won't be in for hours yet," Milly says. "We checked the tide table."

"Come on," Vincent says. He holds up a flashlight. "A good Boy Scout always comes prepared." He laughs.

They follow him in, follow the halo of his flashlight, which seems to become dimmer the further in they go.

"Ferris?" Tanja calls when he stops suddenly.

"Coming." He takes a deep breath and continues.

The earth smells dank, and a frigid air assails him. In front of him, the flashlight's glow recedes ever further, as do Vincent, Milly and Tanja. Ferris looks behind him at the jagged entrance, and the foaming waves against rocks. His breath quickens and he freezes. It takes all his willpower not to panic. He stays still until he feels in control, then slowly makes his way out, and collapses on the sand.

"Are you ok?" Tanja says, as soon as she emerges.

He nods, feeling stupid. He's not supposed to be afraid. Now, he's embarrassed more than anything.

"Milquetoast," Vincent said.

Ferris shrugs and listens to their descriptions of the cave, envious of their excitement and elation. It's as if his heart has stopped, and he's watching himself going through the motions of living.

That night, after supper, Tanja pours his vodka into a tumbler and hands it to him. He takes a gulp, then says, "I'm going to have to go home early."

Tanja frowns. "What's wrong?"

"There's nothing wrong," he says, and sighs. "You can stay on with Vincent and Milly. Finish the trip."

"Then why do you need to go?" Tanja asks.

"It's nothing really…," he says vaguely. He flips on the TV.

She studies him for a moment while he switches channels. "Ferris," she says. "Look at me."

He turns to her.

"What's going on here?" She touches his arm.

"Nothing's going on," he says lamely.

"Maybe that's the problem," Tanja says.

Ferris sighs. "I know. I know. It's not fair to you, but…I'm just not ready at the moment…" He strokes her shoulder. "I'm not saying forever. Maybe —" He knows he's holding out a carrot, trying to soften the blow.

"You're still waiting for Cindy Crawford," she says, her lips pursed, making him regret that he told her the anecdote from his past.

Back home, the next day, he stares at her texts, texts he does not intend to reply to, unless it's from the airport. A hasty goodbye. Then, he'll put the cell into Airport Mode.

o o o

*Absence is a house so vast that inside you will pass through its walls and hang pictures on the air.*

— Pablo Neruda

## COLE

Cole's been flitting between time zones since he was fifteen. He rocks and rolls on stages, on airplanes, in beds with women whose names he can't recall. A guitar prodigy, he was on tour in

Europe with his band Cole Harbour when he was barely out of his teens. In France, he fell in love with a singer, who bore him a child, then died.

He brought the baby home to his sister Fiona, and left her there. He doesn't blame the child — Paris — not exactly, though her life is permanently linked to death in his mind. He should have clung to her, instead of being frightened by her needs. He was too young to care for a child, he told himself. He was too busy. He was always travelling, a permanent tourist in his own life.

Fiona emailed him to remind him of his daughter, her birthdays, her high-school graduation, her university convocation. Sometimes, if he was in a nearby city, he'd rent a car and go visit them, bringing extravagant gifts and signed copies of his album and CD covers, to which he added personal dedications. He turned away from the adoration in his daughter's eyes and spent most of the visit telling them about his road exploits, his famous friends.

After Paris had gone to bed, his sister would ask about the cocaine, the opioids, the alcohol, but he lied and assured her all that was in the past.

If only he could now turn back the clock, he'd spend the important moments with them, he'd take them to France, he'd hire the best oncologist for his sister, he'd sit at her side in palliative care, he'd go to her funeral. How did he become so negligent? And how could Paris continue to love him?

Every few years, at the insistence of his manager and record label, he checks himself into a rehab centre. *Tell us about your childhood*, the therapists say. *Why are you unhappy?* He shakes his head. He's been self-medicating for so long, he can't pinpoint the beginning. What he knows is that he is in transit to somewhere.

o o o

# PERMANENT TOURISTS

*Every heart has its secret sorrows,*
*which the world knows not, and oftentimes*
*we call a man cold, when he is only sad.*

—Henry Wadsworth Longfellow

## RICHARD

Richard owns townhouses and condos on golf courses — Hawaii, Palm Springs, Georgia — summer cottages in Oregon, Maine, New Hampshire. Self-contained, these lock-key houses are complete, with kitchenware, cutlery, framed art, towels and board games, as if the family who lived here had stepped out for the afternoon.

What he carries from place to place as well as underwear and toiletries are Homma Golf's Five Star Set, seven Lyle and Scott polo shirts in various shades of blue with their Golden Eagle logo prominently displayed, Nike's Shield Golf Jacket and Calloway golf shoes.

He is not a particularly good golfer — his score consistently over 100 — though once, years ago, he made a hole-in-one on a Par 3, and since then has elevated his sense of his own aptitude so that he now believes himself to be much better than he is. Each time his score surpasses the 100 mark, he acts surprised, as if this were an exception rather than the rule.

He grew up poor, uneducated, in a rat-infested housing project, his mother a waitress at a nearby bar, his father long gone. A poverty cliché, he tells people. He swore to rise above that darkness, and now owns a thriving business, warehouses full of merchandise, offices in four major cities; a business that no longer needs him. When he began, he worked sixteen-hour days, with no time for holidays or golf or women.

At first, his new-found freedom is a burden, the house empty. He imagines everyone else at home, eating dinner with wives and husbands and children, watching television, their perpetual smiles brightened by teeth-whitening creams, their fridges filled with organic produce, their children cheerful and agreeable, their bedsheets tousled and musty with sex. He goes into the kitchen and opens the fridge. The racks contain a jar of pickles, a plastic ketchup bottle, a half lemon with curled brown edges, a jug of soya sauce, a milk carton, an apple and two bottles of white Chilean wine.

He befriends bartenders, hostesses, wait-staff at the restaurants, golf pros, security guards at the gated communities. He likes to travel, he tells them all, and lists cities and countries beyond his borders, a veritable global list, describes in detail the interiors of the first-class lounges of luxury liners, the grand lobbies of five-star hotels, the plush seats and gourmet dishes in Michelin-starred restaurants, and the penthouses whose heights insulate him from the dark alleys, from the rats still scurrying in his head.

It's inevitable that he would turn to dating sites and chat lines on the web. The women he meets there are flirty and interested in him. What's the name of his company? Where exactly is his Hawaii condo located? They slowly begin to send him photos of themselves, in revealing tops, in skimpy sexy underwear. They ask for photos of his face, his condos, his ocean views. It's a familiar story — a *W5* segment — where the man/woman falls in love with a face, with the promise of happiness, and soon Richard finds himself in a virtual relationship with a twenty-three-year-old, who is always in the midst of a crisis that requires money, which he sends. She lives across the world from him, and though he offers to fly her over, or to go visit her, she always manages an excuse at the last moment so he never actually meets her face to face. He emails her every day, and late at night, he Skypes her into his bedroom, where he can fantasize her near him, and hear her enthusiastic sexual sighs.

In the daytime, he circuits his townhouses and condos. Sometimes, nostalgia propels him to visit his former self in a strip mall outside of Vegas, where he has a rented storage locker filled with his collections of stamps, coins, tobacco tins, postcards, T-shirts, old vinyl records, high school yearbooks and vintage signs. In a room in the motel across the street, he sifts through the old mementos, while his younger self trickles like sand between his fingers. It's as pointless as going to a rock concert to see a band he loved two decades before, a band whose lyrics no longer reflect him. He roams golf courses, eats at the club restaurants, and at night settles in his king-sized bed, alone.

One evening, in response to his email, he gets a "Postmaster @" undeliverable message. He searches frantically for his twenty-three-year-old in chatlines and dating sites, but she has vanished, along with a considerable amount of his money. He Googles her name, the dating site, adds "missing," as if he thinks she may have been abducted. The search renders 650 pages of Romance Scams. He shudders at the thought of himself as victim. How could he have been so stupid? Soon, he receives a phone call, a request for an interview, and before long, he is in front of a detective, who wants his co-operation. The police have been following this couple — a conman and his girlfriend — for the past year. The newspapers do a story, and suddenly Richard is unravelled and reduced to a dupe, a foolish empty chump.

o o o

## Support Group

Ellen sits, her arms crossed, her travel bag hanging on the back of her chair.

"What can you achieve," Dr. Aña Delgado says, "immobile at home?"

The others stare at Ellen, waiting. All around the room are posters of quotes to help them in their journeys towards healing. These seven are united in loss, weighed down by guilt and grief. She leans forward.

Ellen shrugs. What she wants to say is that she's waiting for the knock at the door, the policeman's voice saying they've found Mika. Alive. Cold case solved, like a suitcase found in the snow. Instead, she says, "I'm not hurting anyone." Her eyes move to the poster Dr. Delgado made for her: *Sometimes, only one person is missing, and the whole world seems depopulated.* That's exactly how she feels.

Dr. Delgado gives her a questioning look. Two of the others nod. Ellen likes to imagine her child lost her way or was spirited into a foreign country, and if she keeps watching the documentaries, she'll spot her on a street and they'll be reunited, like the Indian boy Saroo in the movie *Lion*. Or maybe Joyce will find Mika. That can't be too much to hope for. "I need to keep her alive," she says.

And now several of them shift in their chairs; their eyes beam sympathy, support. They'd all be happy for a miracle to solve grief, to be a counterweight to loss, to rescue their misplaced selves.

"No one is suggesting you forget your daughter," Dr. Delgado says, "but rather that you learn to live with the loss."

Ellen frowns. "Anyway," she adds. "They might still find her. Miracles do happen."

Vivian shifts in her seat beside Ellen. "I wish," she says. She wants to believe in miracles, but knows nothing will bring her sister back. *Grief is like the ocean; it comes on waves ebbing and flowing. Sometimes the water is calm, and sometimes it is overwhelming. All we can do is learn to swim.*

Dr. Delgado beams her a sympathetic smile. Vivian blames herself for her half-sister's death, though she was living in Toronto at the time.

"If only I'd known," Vivian says, thinking she was on holiday when it happened. The phone call came days later, from a government worker looking for a next-of-kin. To add to her guilt, she inherited all her sister's possessions, including the Vancouver house. Vivian left her job in Toronto, her friends, her mother, and now lives in Vancouver, carrying the terrible burden of Marissa's suicide.

Ferris turns the worry stone over and over in his palm. "How could you have known?" he says.

Vivian shrugs.

Ferris doesn't expect an answer; he just wants to be supportive — isn't that the point of these meetings? But he doesn't believe in miracles. And he doesn't really believe that talking to a group of strangers every week can solve anything, though he's been meeting with this group for the past six months, so technically they're not strangers. Hard as he tries, however, he can't engage with their sorrows, won't let them overwhelm him. Compounding sorrow, he thinks, is a tidal wave, violent, dangerous. He fears the tsunami, the acceleration, the debris of guilt, the currents, the engulfment.

Dr. Delgado turns to him. "What steps have you taken to move forward?"

He looks across the room at his poster: *The reality is you will grieve forever… you will rebuild yourself around the loss. You will be whole again but you will never be the same.* It's all well and good to say these things, but quite another to live them. How is he to be whole again, knowing he was driving that car? The group watches him. They've all had their turn at pseudo-analyzing his inability to form lasting connections. They've suggested he join a country or a tennis club, that he go to a matchmaker, that he take up gardening, golfing, cooking, painting, etc. What they don't seem to understand is that he's not looking for something to do, and he's not unhappy being single… or maybe he is. Their suggestions, however, sound absurd in his ears. He doesn't share their cheerful optimism for him, given that they lack this same optimism for their own lives.

He looks at Dr. Delgado, who smiles. "I prefer my own company," he says, defensively. "I like being self-contained."

Self-contained? How is that different from walled in, trapped? Richard thinks. The words "self-contained" echo in the air. He's uttered them himself many times. After their last session, he went for a drink with Ferris, who tried to convince him that relationships are not all that important in the natural order of things. In fact, according to Ferris, men should carry on with the important things in life (this being production) and relegate a small amount of time, say thirty minutes a day, to the upkeep of their personal relationships. This would remove all need and dependence on the other person. Richard half-heartedly agreed, in principle, at least. What Ferris was suggesting was a life of total control; of freedom from the shackles of emotions and commitments. It does occur to him that Ferris, for all his talk, is far from an example of this theory at work. Ferris's relationships (if one could even call them that) last on the average one to three weeks. But he is convincing in his argument, citing the pleasures and advantages of single life to offset any questions. Richard needs to believe what Ferris told him; he needs to believe that he can retake total control of his life and this, in Ferris's terms, means that he will not invest any time or energy in another person. Not, at least, to the extent that he invested in his online con.

In his real life, however, he would like to be comfortable around CEOs, CFOs, all those Chiefs who frequent the same venues as he does. He invests in the identical companies, buys houses in desirable neighbourhoods, belongs to ritzy country clubs, wears the same brands of clothes, practises things to say, yet he can't shake the feeling that they're judging him, and that he doesn't measure up.

"Maybe you're projecting your own feelings," Denise, the youngest of the group says. "Maybe that's not how they see you at all."

"And maybe they do," Richard says, thinking it's better to be independent, self-reliant, a self-made man who needs no one. He has swallowed his words for so long that he has developed an unconscious disconcerting habit of dry swallowing whenever he comes across anything disagreeable, so that his Adam's apple twitches up and down like an early warning system. Those who do not know him notice only that he stands rigidly and holds his head slightly forward, as if ready to speak, the result of which has plagued him with a permanent crick in his neck. If he could speak about all this, he would tell everyone about the way the words coil into tight fists in his stomach, and how they unleash inside him unexpectedly, the venom manifesting as chronic bleeding ulcers.

As he struggles to speak, Dr. Delgado nods. She understands how mortified and embarrassed he feels, his private life made public, a spectacle of weakness. *Every heart has its secret sorrows, which the world knows not, and oftentimes we call a man cold, when he is only sad.* The others avoid his eyes. He'd willed his mother everything, left a note, hadn't blamed anyone but himself. Yet that weakness — the 911 call. Dr. Delgado pats his hand. Richard sighs. He has been surfing through life, never touching water. And no one needs him.

"I think we all project our own feelings," Denise insists.

"Perhaps so," Dr. Delgado says. At twenty-four, Denise is struggling to reconcile her feelings for her father — a serial philanderer, whose wife has welcomed him back each time with open arms. She's here because her high school sweetheart broke up with her, precipitating a crisis her mother worried might lead to self-harm.

"Everything was perfect, and then he just left," Denise tells them. She thinks of her childhood diary, the "relevant narratives" now locked away in a box in the basement of her parents' house. "It's like he carved a hole in my heart," she says. She takes a tissue out of her purse and dabs her eyes.

"*Remembrance of things past is not necessarily the remembrance of things as they were,*" Dr. Delgado quotes. "Try to recall your last year before the breakup. Memory is a very fluid thing. Selective."

"That's so true," Clara says, "I can see it in my own life." She points to her poster quote: *Mostly it is loss which teaches us about the worth of things.*

Dr. Delgado smiles. Clara has come a long way in the past six months. Newly divorced after years of marriage to a man old enough to be her father, a man who convinced her he deserved credit for her accomplishments, she's beginning to believe in her own worth.

Cole nods. That's how he feels too. Losing everything has made him see the worth of people. He spent a life nourished by an entourage of agents, managers, groupies, freeloaders, eager to supply whatever he needs — k-pins, roofies, jellies, zannies, liquid E, catha, blotter, topi, magic mushrooms, purple rain, half moon, little smoke, mexican tar, stardust, speedball, apple jacks, crystal meth, smack, oxycet, tootsie rolls, oxagons, trammies, and alcohol to chase it up or down — an entourage on payroll.

"Of course, it's my own fault," he says. "I see that," the dependency, the need excruciating. He is a classic case of rock star rags-to-riches-to-rags. Now fifty-four, his star diminished by too many missed concerts, alcoholic stage rants, a manager who mishandled his finances, he is trying to understand where he took the wrong turn. *Absence is a house so vast that inside you will pass through its walls and hang pictures on the air.* He has alienated everyone. How can he be a better person when he hardly knows himself?

*Greater things are believed of those who are absent.*

—Tacitus

# BLOODLINES

The first email is brief, no details. The man wishes to locate a relative, long abandoned by the family, his only link to the past. Can she send him a quote?

Paris wonders what he hopes to find. A stranger to change the course of his life? Supplant his identity, his loyalties?

Open on her desk lies the file of her current client, who is in for a surprise. Paris often uncovers irregularities in family trees, and she is bound by professional ethics to disclose secrets people have guarded throughout their lives: barren women who clandestinely adopted children; women whose circumstances forced them to give theirs away to be raised by others; war brides whose children belong to the dead, not to the husbands who raised them; and now, increasingly, children born of sperm donors, some of whom want to be acknowledged in family lines.

In this case, the client is a young woman whose surname, Plantagenet, conjures illustrious ancestors, and who has, by her own admission, consulted a fortune teller, and now believes that in a past life, she was Katherine Plantagenet, the illegitimate daughter of Richard III. Paris sighs. Why are so many people confident that they derive from royal or famous lineage? She's never met anyone who claims a humble past life. Ordinary persons, apparently, are not reincarnated, if such a thing exists. Paris sighs again and closes the file. Tomorrow, she will have to inform the young woman that her great-great-great grandfather's name was "Plank," probably acquired by living near a plank bridge in England. On his arrival in Canada, he adopted the name Plantagenet to better his circumstances.

Three days a week, Paris works at the main library as an archivist, a natural progression of her education — her life flowing from one thing to another with few impediments, as if she were destined to be exactly where she is. From high school to university, from an undergraduate degree in anthropology to a master's degree in archival studies, from town to city. Over the years, she has completed online courses with the National Institute for Genealogical Studies, has compiled a multitude of family histories — her own included — and after her CG accreditation, has gone into business for herself, a business she pursues on a part-time basis, from her home office in a one-bedroom-and-den condo overlooking the railyards and beyond those, the Vancouver harbour. From her tiny balcony she has an unobstructed view of the mountains' burst of green, the billowing waves nudging the opposite shore; and in darkness, the ascending rows of streetlights scaling the mountain's ankles, the ski run constellations in the night sky, the obsidian sea, studded here and there with the festive sparkle of lights outlining ships awaiting entrance to the harbour.

On her days off, for the past two years, Paris has driven to a lockdown facility 200 kilometres away to visit her once larger-than-life father, who inexplicably spiralled into early Alzheimer's in his late fifties, the same father who, after her mother's death in childbirth, deposited Paris with a maiden aunt and went on the road with his band. For years, he was a successful rock star, his videos garnering millions of views, his songs on *Billboard's* top-100. Throughout her teens, Paris loved him fervently from afar, obsessively streaming his singles and YouTube videos. Then came drugs and alcohol. She evaded her friends' questions and denied his self-destruction, comebacks and relapses documented in technicolour detail in the gossip magazines she cringed at when in grocery stores.

When the social worker first contacted her to determine whether Paris could and would take her father in, Paris was overjoyed and eager. She imagined the two of them finally getting to know each other. When the arrangement was approved, she moved into a larger apartment, bought new towels and bed linen. However, the father who returned to where he'd never been was frail and disoriented, his forehead etched into a frown, his cheeks gaunt and ashen, his eyes bright in a circle of grey, as if he'd been shooting up for days. He had been hospitalized for injuries sustained in a fight outside a bar, the social worker told her, and as a result had had a battery of tests that confirmed the diagnosis. He was aware of his condition, frustrated by his confusion, raging against invisible gods, fate, anyone near him. In the privacy of her bedroom late at night, Paris scrolled through dementia sites, trying to understand what her father was experiencing. Already, she realized, he was somewhere between the third and fourth stage. Some evenings, he'd ask her the same question over and over, and she'd answer in even tones, which only briefly satisfied him. He began to fret about appointments, unsure of the times and dates, and no matter how much she tried to reassure him, he was agitated. He'd borrow her car and forget it in parking lots. One day, he looked at his guitar and asked her who played it. Another day, he dressed for a grocery store outing in a silver lamé pantsuit. Paris had to gently lead him back to his room and lay out appropriate clothes on his bed — something she began to do daily. She hid the car keys.

Finally, two years ago, when he was brought home by a police officer because he didn't know his name or address, Paris gave in to the social worker's insistence that he be placed in care. At the lockdown, his condition deteriorated quickly, so that often he didn't even recognize her. That was the worst of it — to be near him as a stranger, his eyes indifferent and uncaring. She cried after every visit, her cheeks wet, her eyes red, enraged by the unfairness of it. She had imagined a rosy future for them together. Those nights, her tears soaked her pillow, as she wept rivers of grief, self-pity, and nostalgia for their ghost life.

In her real life, Paris is inexplicably drawn to certain people, due, perhaps, to a recognition of an unspoken similar past. The other night, for example, she'd watched a BBC online video featuring an interview with a medium, a young woman in her late twenties, blonde hair, blue eyes, dressed in black leggings and a pale apricot sweater. She did not resemble Paris's imagined medium: clad in black, eyes ringed in kohl, long slate hair and a fringed shawl. No, this young woman called herself "a traveller and a spiritual guidance counsellor." She had recently returned from Australia, where she claimed to have fallen in love with a ghost.

"Tell us what you talk about," the TV host said, gamely trying to suspend his disbelief.

She paused. "Well, we don't…talk like… it's more of a feeling… an emotion. It's very hard to explain, but we are totally connected."

"And you say you fell in love? Can you tell us how this happened?" the TV host said, through a half smile.

"Yes, I was in Australia, and while I was walking through the forest one day, he found me." She turned and smiled, as if to reassure the ghost beside her.

"And then?"

"Well," she said, "normally spirits are static, so I was very sad when I had to leave him." She smiled shyly. "But when I was on the plane home, there he was!"

"What, physically?"

"No, of course not," she said. "I can't see him. But it's just like a human relationship otherwise." She smiled again. "But we did go into the washroom…and joined the mile-high club."

The TV host leaned forward. "What if you are just imagining this?"

"I know it's real," she said firmly. "And I don't mind if people disbelieve."

"What's next then? Marriage? A baby?"

"We're planning a handfasting—that's the old term, essentially, for a spiritual marriage. A promise. As to the baby, well, there are many phantom pregnancies, and I believe these are real, in that they produce ghost babies."

"So you think you'll have a ghost baby?" the TV host said, frowning.

"I don't know whether it will be a physical baby or..."

"Well, good luck to you and your ghost lover," the TV host said.

Paris felt immediate empathy for this young woman, as one would for a lonely child with an imaginary friend.

A ghost lover, Paris thinks, is a very attractive prospect: no back talk, no messy scenes, no unpleasantness. One can conjure and banish him at will, unlike a real man, like her ex, Dean, who resists being conjured, who doesn't answer his phone and who certainly would never follow her onto a plane. In fact, after six months of what Paris thought was a relationship, he has abruptly broken up with her, citing vague excuses, inside which she hears *goodbye*.

In the second email, the man acknowledges her fee, includes his mother's maiden name — Agnes Delores Basten — and writes that he's seeking his mother's younger sister, who when discovered pregnant at fifteen, was cast out of the family. She had been the youngest of ten children, twenty-one years younger than her oldest sibling. He has no idea whether she married or not, or what her name would have become. In fact, he only discovered this sister's existence after his mother's death, in a grainy black-and-white photograph, which his mother labelled on the back as "Father, Mother, Miriam and me." Then at a later time, she'd pencilled "my sister" above the word "Miriam." The man believes his mother wanted him to find this phantom sister, stricken from the family out of misplaced shame.

"That's so sad," Paris's friend Zoë says, without looking up from her iPhone, when Paris tells her about this latest client. They're sitting in the corner booth at The Crowsnest, a favourite evening rendezvous, a British-style pub/lounge retrofitted with oak panelling and bookshelves filled with wooden painted book spines.

"Why sad?" Paris says. "I don't think it's sad. I think it's great." She glances around the room, at the many people all staring at their phones. In the library, too, Millennials sit at cubicles or stand among racks, surrounded by books, yet their eyes are constantly focused on their phones and tablets. They're distracted when spoken to, their thumbs hammering out words like pestles pounding rock salt. Though they take up physical space in the library, they are elsewhere, following the trajectory of their alter-egos to other invented selves, as if this life were too dull compared to the ones inside their phones. Paris wonders if at home they turn off their phones and have conversations with their loved ones. She knows it's difficult to disconnect from the intoxication of likes and followers, to think one's voice is heard and matters. She sighs. "What's sad about wanting to feel connected to something that goes back generations, instead of hours?"

"Family connections are highly overrated." Zoë swipes through men's faces on her phone, pausing now and then on one that pleases her. The pseudo banker's lamp huddling on their table bathes her face in a green eerie glow.

"One-night hookups are highly overrated," Paris says, thinking she's had her share of them, mostly with musicians. She leans back into the upholstered brown pleather of their booth.

"Maybe so, but you can choose. And you can get rid of them when you want. Can't do that with family."

"You don't always get to choose."

"Actually," Zoë says, looking up, "you *do* get to choose." She sets her phone face down on the table. "There are plenty of good men out there. But you choose the bad boys, and guess what? That's what they turn out to be."

Paris shrugs. She's heard this lecture before, from Zoë, from her aunt Fiona when she was alive, even from her father years ago. Men, he told her, are not feral dogs to be tamed. Go for one that's already tame. But she has always loved the wild ones, their unpredictability, their mood swings. They are unfulfilled promises, hope. Tame men are like domesticated dogs, panting, curled at one's feet, desperate for fleeting shows of affection. No, the wild boys, the bad boys are untamable and that makes them exotic and desirable. Dean is simply the latest in a long line of dingoes.

She excuses herself and goes to the washroom, to get away from Zoë's well-intentioned advice — advice Zoë herself does not follow, given that for years, she's been having an affair with a married man in Calgary. What Zoë could possibly be getting out of this non-relationship since she returned to live in Vancouver is anyone's guess, though Paris imagines the all-expenses-paid trips, the mini-vacations and tennis bracelets have something to do with it. She wonders if this semblance of a relationship suits Zoë best. She can be both single and committed. She can pine and window-shop. Zoë's as close to Paris as one who is not a blood relative can be. In their teens, they covered for each other when they were dating bad boys, frequenting forbidden dives, smoking and experimenting with various pharmaceuticals. They were secretive and loyal. Despite this history, the major difference that defines them is that Zoë has living parents, a sister, uncles and aunts, first and second cousins, who congregate for family dinners on holidays and birthdays, who are genuinely happy to be in each other's company.

For a moment, Paris catches a glimpse of herself in the mirror — bare, frightened, an orphan.

She takes out her cellphone, but there is no one to call.

When she returns, their friend Skye has joined them. A peanut bowl overflows on the table in front of them, and wine-glasses sweat around Zoë and Skye's fingers. The large flat-screen TVs mounted around the bar are all tuned to the BBC, which, instead of sports, now play and replay footage of a minor reality-TV star who overdosed, along with the mass hysterical response to her death — women sobbing in the streets; young men holding bouquets of flowers; mounds of cards and teddy bears laid at the hospital entrance; even the journalists, unable to keep their voices from quavering.

Paris feels an overwhelming urge to cry along with everyone. She thinks of her father slowly losing himself, of the tenuous bonds that bind people, that bind memory to the self.

"It's nuts," Zoë says. "Absurd. Hundreds of people die every day from war, disease, displacements. Why should we care about a reality-TV star who overdosed?"

"I think it's tragic," Skye says.

"We're not talking Othello here," Zoë says, a small edge to her voice.

In the midst of this, Dean walks in, dressed impeccably, as always, as if he were ready to step onto a catwalk at London's Fashion Week, his blond mane shiny and lustrous. He's a race car driver whose bed she fell into, aroused by his recklessness, the speed and danger, the grin in the post-race interviews. In real life, he was taciturn and unpredictable, and to her, these extremes were possibilities of unleashed desire.

"Hey, there's Fabio," Zoë says, raising her hand to motion him over. Zoë did a feature on him for a new magazine, and introduced him to Paris at the launch.

Paris cringes, and holds her arm. "No. Don't."

Zoë turns, startled. "You're in the middle of a fight," she says.

"What happened?" Skye asks, frowning. "Did you break up?"

Paris's cheeks are burning. She reaches for a handful of peanuts and eats them, staring at the piano player beyond them. When she can trust herself, she says, "There's nothing to tell, really." And it's true. This *break* is exactly that, a break, not an interruption but a fracture slowly widening to crevasse.

Dean turns towards a table where a tall thin brunette smiles at his approach. He has already moved on, Paris thinks, and this is a peacock show. The woman's face glows with delight, her mouth a small rainbow upcurve. Paris wonders if this woman sits with him and watches his favourite YouTube videos of bullfights and bronc riding, or if she's like Paris, perturbed over these subjugation videos society condones and labels entertainment. She wonders why her friends possess great bullshit detectors, while she always falls.

Dean raises his hand in a small wave.

"What a jerk," Zoë says. "He knows you come here." She glares in Dean's direction, but he's leaning towards the brunette.

"Let's go somewhere else," Skye says, and they all slide out of the booth. "Asshole," she hisses in Dean's direction.

Paris looks back at Dean and the brunette, wondering if she had looked that happy at first, thinking about how quickly things shift. A careless word. An impassive gesture. Like a summer storm, sun to rain in the split of thunder.

In the third email, the man writes to say he wants to send Paris his mother's papers, in case she can find something he missed. His name is Thomas, and he lives a four-hour drive from the city.

She emails the library's address and tells him she has not been able to trace his aunt. Perhaps the young woman changed her name in order to disappear. She asks the man — Thomas — for more specific information regarding the family, their movements through the years, etc. A young woman, banished from home, might endeavour to keep track of her family, even as she conceals herself, like a pyromaniac compelled to watch the effects of her fire, or a murderer returning to the scene of her crime. The woman was born into a culture that shamed women's desire. Not much has changed, Paris thinks. Only the medium. She wonders if the woman was abandoned by the father of her child, or whether she eventually linked up with him and moved away; whether she raised the child alone or with a new partner. She considers asking Thomas for a DNA sample, though unless Miriam or her child had their DNA extracted and uploaded it to a genealogy site, she wouldn't be able to match it.

When the man's papers arrive, she sorts through them for clues. Is Thomas searching bloodlines for who he is or for who he wants to be? The Greeks considered blood to be the same as soul or psyche, a source of life, of spirit. Is his longing about mortality, or the fear of being left alone in the world? Or is he yearning, perhaps, for a tangible connection at a time when human connection is both constant and non-existent?

She examines hospital records and baptism certificates, church ledgers, immigration records, census records, military records, land records, and government-created records. She searches heritage sites and traces internet links. She checks city directories as well as communities and local histories within 500 kilometres of where Thomas lives. The stack of files on her desk are tunnels she mines for *bloodline, clan, descendant, tribe*. However, all she finds is what she already knows: the phantom aunt existed, at least until her mid-teens. No death certificates match her name, no obituaries attest to her life. And her child, if she had one, has also disappeared into a ghost trail of absence.

At the lockdown, her father befriends an energetic older woman named Darlene, whose dementia is less advanced than his. Paris often finds Darlene with her father, chatting or simply sitting with him in silence. Both veer in and out of memory, as if wayfaring, reaching for signposts and cornerstones of experiences, mapping their youths, decisions, the homes they inhabited, the cities visited, the lockdown rooms and terrifying spells of oblivion that overtake them unannounced.

Beyond the fence of the lockdown perimeter are railway tracks that extend into the distance. Several times a day, when a unit train reverberates past, her father thinks he's at a rock concert. "Turn down the damn bass!" he shouts to the soundman in his head. "I can't hear myself."

Darlene pats his arm, reassures him. "He's turning it down, Cole. See? It's better already." Darlene has no family, no visitors. Sometimes, she stares at Paris wistfully. "You're a good daughter," she says. "I wish you were my daughter." Other times she dismisses Paris as if she were a troublesome neighbour.

Often, she says, "He'll remember you next time," while Paris sits, despairing over her father's impassiveness. "He loves you, and love will bring back his memory."

This sounds warm and fuzzy to Paris, but she doesn't believe a word of it.

Sometimes her father nods as if he does remember her, and for a blissful moment she believes it's all a frightful mistake, and they will retrieve their former lives; no, they will create new ones.

However, as the months pass, try as she might, she can't coax her father to recall the two of them. How could he have forgotten the night of his concert in the Colosseum, where Paris, Aunt Fiona and Zoë prowled immense underground passages, as if they were wild beasts waiting to be released; musicians and roadies sprawled on leather couches, grazed buffets laden with delicacies, bent over pool tables, leaned on bar countertops; security guards ushered them through as if they were in a James Bond film, privy to secret entryways and delights. How could he not recall singing to them, calling out Paris's name, and leading her to the mic, where she was blinded by spotlights and emotion, by the arena's immense sky flickering with thousands of mini lights, echoing Paris's flickering heart? Her father's arm steadied her while they sang together, and in that moment, she forgave him everything and was only aware of the two of them in harmony, together, his light shining on her like a supernova.

How could he have forgotten that? How could he have forgotten her? It's as if their life were an accidental photograph, and he has burned out her image, turned her into a jagged void. Love alone will not bring back any memory.

Sometimes, her father paces back and forth, shaking his head. He leans towards Darlene and asks "Who is that?" in a stage whisper that chills Paris's blood.

"Dad, it's me. Paris," she says, trying to reassure him.

Most often than not, he shrinks from her, eyes her suspiciously. "I have no daughter," he says, his arm dismissing her, and she remembers the ending of that story, how during their final notes, the arena exploded into thunderous applause. If she closes her eyes, she can return to it now, the audience's whistles, the lighters held high, turning the arena into a constellation. Why hadn't she understood that the applause was for her father, that she was a trick he'd produced? And later that night, when he took her to an upscale restaurant, the lavish attention she basked in was for the benefit of the journalists and photographers, who loved this father-daughter angle, who photographed them and interviewed him, and asked him questions about the difficulty of raising a daughter, as if he had. Later still, when she asked him if now she would be travelling with him, he smiled and patted her head.

The next morning he was gone.

Out of the blue, Dean begins to email her, telling her he misses her, that he's made a terrible mistake, that she is his soulmate, that he can't live without her, etc.

"What I find interesting," Zoë says, "is that you seem to be shying away from real emotions." She picks up an eyeshadow palette, and holds it up to Paris's face.

"What do you mean?" Paris asks. She's been saying that although she hasn't yet responded to Dean's texts and emails, she finds his persistence intriguing. She feels wanted.

She, Zoë and Skye are in a spa, sitting in two beautician's chairs, awaiting makeovers — *A natural look! Let us make you a better version of yourself!* — rotating in soothing half-circle rhythms. Paris shrugs, because there's no point trying to explain that head and heart are not connected, that she both agrees and disagrees, that she chose this drama and subjected herself to endless humiliations in the name of love. This is what makes life interesting — the ambiguities. If Dean had been a perfect human being, she'd probably not be interested in him.

One of the beauticians picks up a remote and flicks on the flat-screen. "Hope you don't mind," she says, but they're going to show some of Meghan and Harry's wedding." She doesn't wait for a response, and soon the actress appears stepping out of a limo. "A real princess wedding," the beautician says wistfully.

Paris stares at the elegant white gown and veil, half-envious of the fairy-tale future being implied, though she knows life isn't that simple.

"You are a complete dolt," Skye says. "I can't believe you're actually considering taking Dean back, despite what he did to you." She twirls a rope of hair around her finger, making a ringlet.

"Didn't do, you mean," Zoë says.

"That was months ago," Paris says.

"So what's changed?" Skye says.

Why Paris would give Skye any credence on the subject of love is beyond any conjecture, given that she has a history of romances with avatars she meets in Second Life — avatars who Paris thinks resemble cartoon characters, elongating everyone's childhood into eternity. Skye dates them in Second Life, and breaks up with them in Second Life — a very convenient way to live out a series of dangerous and banal fantasies in a parallel world to this real, very messy one.

"You need to deal with your father issues," Zoë says.

*Father issues.* The words roil in Paris's head. A stack of father issues, like periodicals recurring at regular intervals.

"Don't come looking for sympathy if you take him back," Skye says.

"I didn't say I was going to," Paris says lamely, thinking about her history with boyfriends and lovers — interludes in the true sense of the word — short dramatic passages connecting and contrasting the rest of her life. Brief, episodic.

She continues to drive to the lockdown twice a week despite her father's descent into silence. Precarious as their relationship has been, now that he's lost to himself, Paris, too, feels untethered, disconnected. Despite her passion for genealogy, she feels no relief in knowing her grandparents were x and y, living in such-and-such a town, country, continent. She researched both her father and mother's lineage back to several European destinations, which she has not visited, and doesn't know whether distant relatives still inhabit those faraway cities. But without memory — without the personal narratives that would connect her to them — her ancestors could be anyone. She needs the similarities, the soul, the spirit within the bloodstream.

One day, she arrives and her father is agitated, trying to tell her something important. He leans into her, and she into him. He begins a sentence, then falters and stops, as if afraid of divulging some terrible secret. "Your mother," he whispers, "has been hiding all these years." Paris holds her breath, waiting for him to continue, but soon he devolves into recounting the plot of a film that recently aired on television, albeit with himself and her mother as protagonists. It both shocks and saddens Paris, to think that without memory, one's identity can dissolve, and that new stories can supplant memories, form new identities.

The idea comes to her out of this. What if she can link Thomas and Darlene? For a long time, she considers the ethics — or rather, the lack of ethics — of it. What harm could she do by bringing together two people who long to connect? What difference does it make whether they share a bloodline or not? She begins to research Darlene's genealogy. Born in 1932, she is the only child of a missionary and his wife, both of whom died of congestive heart failure, a few months apart, possibly due to Chagas disease they had contracted while in South America decades earlier. Darlene trained as a nurse, was never married, nor had children. Research uncovers no Facebook profile, no Twitter handle, no social media activity of any kind (how has she managed to move about everyday life, Paris wonders). Darlene's name is scattered in nursing directories, on the list of needle-exchange volunteers, mentioned on a hospital site with the date of her retirement party, as if her life has been whitewashed for web use. In short, she's the perfect candidate for an identity makeover.

Paris is at home after work, on the couch, scrolling through twelve grainy photos of Dean at the racetrack, in front of a pit stop, clowning, brooding, smiling, all shot on her cell, when her phone rings.

"Your father has had a fall," the lockdown manager says.

She arrives late at night, and rushes into her father's empty room. Too late. Too late.

The manager of the facility describes the fall, probably caused by a stroke, says words like *didn't suffer, it was quick, DNR, it's for the best.* Paris nods, thinking yes it's true, trying as hard as she can to hold on to that lifeline, that bloodline, even as she feels herself shipwrecked, floating like flotsam on the surface of waves, abandoned to their rhythms, in swirling waters, savage seas. In the morgue, he is both her father and a stranger, his brow no longer frowning, his face relaxed, his eyes lifeless.

She walks out into the dark night, and instead of going to her car in the parking lot, walks towards the train station, unprepared for the silence, the emptiness, wickets closed, no one around, through the building to the platform. Along one track, an electronic board displays the arrival of the next train: 12:45 a.m. She sighs and sits on one of the filthy, graffitied benches. She isn't planning to go anywhere. She only wants to be around strangers, to feel herself surrounded yet apart.

"Attention: Direct train en route to Calgary approaching on Platform 1. Exercise caution. Please stand behind the yellow line. Attention...."

The rumble of a train fills her head, erasing memory and time. She watches the brilliant orb bore through the dark, stands up, moves to the edge of the track. Within seconds, a wind presses against her face, and a blur of red and grey speeds past, in the deafening scrape of metal on metal. Exhilarated, she pushes her breath out all at once; she was not planning to jump. She was simply trying to feel more alive.

Back home, she showers, changes, then sits on the couch, tearless. Her father's death was not unexpected. A part of her relieved that he is free from himself. Yet there's so much she yearns to ask him, so much she doesn't know. She turns on the TV to hear the sound of human voices, and clicks channel to channel, up to 900 and back to 2. The endless selection of mindless chatter depresses her. She clicks and clicks through the numbers again. The cartoon commercials depress her. She clicks and clicks a third round, past medication ads for headaches, erectile dysfunction, arthritis, all followed by a long nightmarish list of negative side effects. She clicks and clicks a fourth round. The reality-TV's star pre-death face appears on seven different channels.

Beyond the plate-glass windows, cargo ships ride at anchor in the harbour; gantry cranes are silhouetted against yellow sulphur mounds; gulls swoop in the air; cars race along the

Lions Gate bridge; people walk to and from work or home or wherever else they're going; everything and everyone moving; everything and everyone a galaxy away. She takes out her phone.

On Facebook, her circled face stares back, beside the words: *What's on your mind?*

"Where has everybody gone?" she types.

Her father's death is broadcast on radio and TV, in newspapers and gossip magazines, on blogs and social media posts. He is suddenly resurrected, remembered, his brilliance celebrated, his falls from grace minimized and justified. The tragedy of a luminous star in his prime struck down by an act of God. Nowhere is a daughter mentioned.

Paris goes through the motions of funeral arrangements, choosing cremation over burial, in a private ceremony only she attends. Her father's former manager arranges the public memorial — "Fans want to pay their respects," he tells her, though she thinks it's all about album sales.

Zoë accompanies her to the green room, as if they were attending a concert instead of a wake. It seems fitting for her father's last public appearance. Paris has been dry-eyed through it all, having mourned her father for the past five years, while he was alive and not living. In the closed-circuit TV mounted on one wall, she sees a multitude of strangers taking their seats. There are familiar faces also: the bartender from The Crowsnest, Skye, clients, colleagues from the library, and Dean alone. In retrospect, she can now pinpoint the exact moment Dean started ebbing from her. She'd been taking her temperature every day. She had even, for a moment, almost succumbed to superstition, considering love potions using menstrual blood to ensure his everlasting loyalty. "You can't be serious," Dean had said. "I'm not ready to be a father."

She stares at his image now, impassive, her grief larger than petty love affairs, more profound, yet calm too.

Finally, the manager ushers them into the hall, where on a stage, a large photo of Paris's father leans on an easel beside a microphone. He is the father Paris revered, the wild boy playing the customized Fifties Fender Stratocaster, bleached blue eyes staring directly at the camera. Two flat-screens project the photo, so that it's in triplicate.

Various people approach the microphone: record producers, band members, studio musicians, roadies, groupies, concert promoters, etc. Some tell clichéd road stories of hijinks and drunken parties; others project a brilliant musician whose light is now spent. No one mentions the drugs, the rehabs. Then a pale, slender young woman slowly advances to the front. She's dressed in black—a knee-length dress, motorcycle jacket, sling-back pumps, and has flaxen hair and large brown eyes that dart from person to person. She stands at the mic, silent, for half a minute, and has everyone's attention.

"I didn't know Cole the way all of you knew him," she says. "I met him seven years ago in a support group. We were all dealing with loss in some way. Cole was an alcoholic, who had lost his wife, and who sabotaged his own life repeatedly. He was a kind, thoughtful man, who wanted to be a better person." She stops here, and quickly walks back to her seat. The air is thick with the unspoken.

After an awkward moment, Paris's father's manager approaches the mic. "We're here to remember Cole and his contribution …" and lists accolades—the numbers of top-10 tunes, the platinum albums, the concerts and TV appearances—a eulogistic delivery that alters the room's energy, and returns it to celebratory. Several musicians mount the stage and sing renditions of Paris's father's songs.

Finally, the speeches end and a cash bar opens. Paris stands with Zoë, looking at the field of strangers.

She feels a tap on her shoulder and turns.

"I wanted to introduce myself," the young woman says. "Vivian." She holds out her hand, and Paris takes it. "There are six of us from that group here." She points to the others: three women and two men.

Paris says, "I had no idea…"

"People don't advertise their losses," Vivian says. She waves the others over, so that Paris can meet them all. "Clara, Richard, Denise, Ellen, Ferris."

Paris shakes each of their hands, thinking we all have losses, or have lost ourselves.

They make small talk for a quarter of an hour, then go to dinner together. Paris wants to know more about her father, about them, about their losses. However, there is no earth-shattering moment when one of them divulges something crucial about her father, no matter how much Paris wishes it. He remains true to himself, an enigma, a riddle she cannot solve.

Back home, at the oddest moments, closed windows panic her. She opens them, gasping. Darkness oppresses her. She buys a night-light. Sits on a park bench staring at impromptu volleyball games, dogs arching for Frisbees, which instead of soothing her, appear sinister and ominous. It's as if her retinas have been torn off and replaced with ones that render everything stark. What she swallows hurts in the pit of her stomach. Her chest feels hollow. She thinks of the stories the women told her, of the support group she wishes she could join now. What good would it do to list the losses, to dwell on absence?

Twice a week, Paris continues her drives to the lockdown.

"Tell me again about your sister," she says each time she visits Darlene, who at first stares at her blankly. Little by little, however, encouraged by Paris's small details, she begins to recall an older sister who she didn't know well, because of their age difference. Her name? Yes, Agnes. That's it.

"You've lost track of Agnes," Paris says. "But maybe there are children, nephews and nieces you've never met."

Darlene's eyes stare into the distance, as if trying to recall these ghost children. In time, she accepts these stories Paris feeds her.

"I've been researching Darlene's genealogy," Paris tells the manager of the lockdown facility, almost a year after Thomas's first email. "I believe I've found her nephew." Darlene has been in the facility for three years now. The possibility of a blood connection thrills everyone. The word "family" conjures the same warm and fuzzy of "love will bring back memory." Who wouldn't want a family, without burned-in shadows and dodgy grainy features? A perfect family of colourized, sun-kissed ghost memories.

No one need know, Paris reasons. Without DNA, no one can dispute her findings. She has been thorough, inserting small information into databases, so that a casual check will turn up what she wants. Nowadays, facts are "fluid," they are "alternate." Posted online, they become truths.

She waits until Darlene no longer recognizes her, then contacts Thomas.

She doesn't go to their reunion, but reads the joyous emails from Thomas, who now believes himself to be Darlene's son. He's recreating his own history, his own memories. His mother, he writes, must have adopted her sister's baby. That's why she wanted him to find Miriam, his birth mother. He has taken Darlene out of that facility and moved her to one in his home town.

Paris lies in bed beneath her childhood comforter, her face against the leaves of the jungle vegetation on the cloth, and imagines lions and leopards grazing her skin. The wild boys. She pushes the comforter into a tent and light streams through the worn fibres of the cotton landscape, turns it into a diorama: her father on a Vegas stage years ago, stringing together all the hits of his career. Each tune revives a memory, and she becomes a little girl listening to her father's voice through speakers, close but inaccessible. In the stage lights, her father looks twenty years younger, and she perceives him suddenly not as her dad, but as a musician in his element, his voice and guitar piercing her heart. This is the father she's never known, the father her mother loved. He is no better, no worse, no different than he has ever been. She watches him, bursting with longing, displaced in a virtual fantasy mini-world. She swallows once, twice, determined to contain herself. Slowly she lowers her hands, and the comforter drops softly, in slow motion, billowing with air as it settles over her.

*Of two sisters one is always the watcher,*
*one the dancer.*

—Louise Glück

# REUNION

It's been years since we were all together again, and here we are, trapped in a rental van, like a packaged déjà vu. Dad still clutches his maps and historical guides; Mom is more mollifying than ever, glossing over any misunderstanding; Kari is wearing her happiness mask, and I am...well, vigilant of them all. We are older now, which means that we should all be more mature and less resentful about all that happened years ago. I say we should be, because naturally, we're not. One's nature does not change with time.

It's an anniversary trip — Mom and Dad's sixtieth. Mom arranged the details and lured Kari and me back with promises meant to conjure slow-motion family embraces in fields of yellow daisies, the kind you see in TV commercials for feminine hygiene products. The reality is that when Kari and I saw each other after a decade of silence, we pecked each other on the cheek and acted as if we had spoken yesterday. I say "reality" because this is how we function in this family. As long as we don't speak the truth, all goes well. We are, however, all wary around Kari, who uncannily zeros in on our scars and gleefully rips them open, until we are left raw and bleeding. So far, all is well.

Dad and Mom sit in the bucket seats behind us while I drive and Kari navigates, which really means that she repeats whatever Dad says from the back. I sneak a peek at my phone's GPS.

"Zoë, put your phone away," Dad says, and I sigh and comply. "We'll navigate the old way," he says, "using paper maps and dead reckoning," whatever that means. It's actually freeing not to have technology to distract us. We are more focused on each other, which could turn out to be disastrous.

In Moab, we stop and check into a hotel.

In our room, Kari casually shrugs out of her long-sleeved shirt to expose a ridge of white lines along both wrists. When she sees me staring at them, she opens her purse, takes out dozens of bangles and pulls them over her hands, concealing the scars.

I turn away, busy myself unpacking my pajamas, when what I want to ask is *how recent are those?* Instead, I say, "Are you all right?"

"Of course I'm all right," Kari says, her tone defensive.

I want to believe her, despite the history, despite the fact that Kari has never been all right. She thrives on some edge only she can feel.

"Mom told me your Wonder Woman magazine folded," Kari says. "What's up with that?" She pulls a pink T-shirt over her head.

I shrug. "Change of culture? Doesn't matter."

"I never thought you'd give up," Kari says, her voice suddenly harsh.

"I didn't give up," I say, annoyed. "I moved on. Been there. Done that." I change into a black shirt, kick off my runners and slip into flip-flops.

Kari raises her eyebrows, but I turn away and pick up my purse. "Ready?" I say in my bright voice, and off we go to the dining room.

Later, Kari and I sneak down to the hotel bar — though why I say "sneak down" is beyond me, given that Mom and Dad are sleeping or watching TV in their own room. However, we tiptoe past their door as if we were teenagers once more, sneaking out of our bedroom window.

Downstairs, while we wait for our glasses of wine, Kari leans over confidentially. "Listen," she says, "I didn't want to say anything in front of Mom and Dad, but I'm meeting someone here."

"What do you mean here? Right now?"

"Yeah," she says, and smiles sheepishly.

"Like who?" I ask. We had been on the road for barely two days. How did she have a chance to meet anyone?

"Larry. That's his name." She looks at her watch. "He's on his way here now."

I frown at her. "You've got to be kidding," I say.

"I didn't meet him on the road, if that's what you're thinking. He's a guy I'm seeing back home."

"Well, why isn't he staying back home?" I say. "We're on a family trip here." The last time I saw Kari, she had divorced her husband Charles and was on her way to Hong Kong with a man called Tom, who I think she later married. I'm sure Mom would have told me if Kari were divorced. "What happened to Tom?" I say. "Aren't you married?"

"We were," she says. "I mean we are…but…Anyway, you should talk."

She is referring to my ongoing affair with Lawrence, a married man I've been seeing for the past twelve years. "That's different," I say.

"Oh yeah?" She narrows her eyes at me. "I've been at either end of that different," she says.

I say nothing.

She shrugs. "Anyway, he followed me."

"You mean like a stalker?"

"No. I mean like he misses me."

"How can he miss you when you've barely been gone?" I say. It's just like Kari to create drama where there doesn't need to be any.

"Whatever, she says, "just be nice to him, okay? He's very fragile."

"You've got to be kidding," I say again, shaking my head, wondering what kind of "fragile" she means. Kari has traditionally been the fragile one, unstable. That's her role in our family. Volatile and unpredictable, she keeps us all tiptoeing around her so as not to incur her wrath, careful not to push her over the edge into self-destruction.

"I'm serious," she says. "I know this'll sound strange, but stay with me. Larry turned up in Ottawa some weeks ago, but he has amnesia and has no idea who he is."

"I can't believe you fell for the stupidest pickup line I've ever heard."

She narrows her eyes at me. "It's not a line. It's real."

"You're making this up," I say. "Or he's making this up."

She reaches across and grasps my arm, nails digging in. "Stop it!" she says.

"Stop it!" I say, and pry her fingers off my arm.

The waitress comes by with our wine, and we are both silent for a moment. I wonder what it would be like to have amnesia. Something about it almost appeals to me. It would be like starting over. Blank slate. I wonder also if this Larry has done something terrible, and is now faking amnesia to avoid the repercussions.

"Does he play the piano?" I say, which is an obscure reference, I know, to a story I read years ago — in the mid 2000s — about a man discovered in Britain who had amnesia and did not speak. He was taken to a secure mental health unit in Kent, where translators tried to get through to him. He finally drew a piano, and when put in front of one, played Tchaikovsky for four hours. He became an internet sensation, with people all over the world claiming they knew "Piano Man" was Italian, French, Swedish, Norwegian, Polish, Lithuanian, Latvian, etc. He was someone's father, uncle, brother, lover, business partner, etc. Eventually he was found to be a German man who had lost his job and had boarded a Euro train to England with the object of committing suicide. However, on the beach, he had chickened out, and when approached, had decided not to speak. I tell Kari all this. "So, in the end," I say, "he was a hoax."

"Larry's not like that," Kari says. "He just doesn't know who he is."

"Who does?" I say.

The words are scarcely out of my mouth when a mid-thirties man approaches us. Kari leaps out of her seat and embraces him. They kiss passionately, during which his eyes are open and staring at me. I look down at my drink, thinking, here we go again. Another of Kari's winners.

"So," I say when he's sitting across from me, his arm around Kari, who stares up at him adoringly. "What do you do, Larry?"

He raises his eyebrows at me. "About what?" he says, deliberately avoiding my question.

"No, I mean what do you work at?"

He waves his hand in the air. "I'm sure Kari's explained about the amnesia," he says. He turns to her and smiles, mouthing a silent kiss.

"How do you pay your rent? Even amnesiacs have to live somewhere," I say.

"I've been staying with friends," he says.

"Oh, so you do remember friends," I say. "What exactly don't you remember?"

He rolls his eyes. "If I knew that, I wouldn't have amnesia, now would I?"

"Larry is staying with some friends he made *after* he was discovered to have amnesia." Kari slips her hand into his. "And we're all trying to help him remember."

The server comes by and he orders a Glenfiddich.

"You remember the name of your favourite drink," I say.

He rolls his eyes again, and sighs. "I haven't forgotten the world," he says, "only who I am in it."

This kind of makes sense, in the same way as I've heard people say that someone with Alzheimer's loses short-term memory but not intelligence. I almost like him, because he said he hasn't forgotten the world. I try to imagine what it would be like to forget everything, to have to learn to see anew, to walk, to talk, rebirth.

The server brings our drinks, which Kari signs to our room. I wonder if she bought his plane ticket. How does someone with amnesia get a bank account or a job or money?

I ask Larry if there's anything he recalls about his former life. Is Larry his real name? Can he drive a car? Is there anything that frightens him? I think he should talk to Mom, who not only is a psychologist, but an expert in changing identities. Some years ago, she renamed herself Eclipse, quit her job, and went off searching for herself in New Age goop. Fortunately, she came to her senses for a while and reverted to Betty (which was her former name), then about six years ago, she decided to become a Buddhist and renamed herself Angkasa — the sky. Today, Betty/Eclipse/Angkasa has become Elizabeth, though Dad still calls her Betty.

"Fire," Larry says.

"You remember it, or you're afraid of it?" I ask.

He shrugs, and he looks uncertain, which makes me think he really has amnesia. "Maybe a bit of both," he says. "I get flashes of billowing fire…naturally, it's frightening." He pauses, shakes his head. "I know how to drive a car, but I can't exactly get a licence, can I, if I don't know who I am?"

"Maybe you should go to a police station and get them to check your fingerprints," I say.

"Ha ha," he says.

"I know!" Kari says, sitting up. "Why don't you do your DNA, and then see if you have any DNA relatives. That's how they catch criminals these days, you know. Think about it! Yes, this is what you should do." She leans back, pleased with herself.

He pulls her close and squeezes her. "What if I'm a notorious criminal?" he says, smiling. "A bank robber, or a mobster. I don't think I'd want to know."

"You don't look like a mobster," Kari says. "And you don't have any money, so you can't be a bank robber." She laughs.

I watch them both, wondering what they know about each other. He must be at least ten or fifteen years younger than Kari. I hope he isn't taking advantage of her, though I know Kari is no wallflower. It's others who should worry around her.

We sit through two more drinks, then when I go to the washroom, Kari follows me.

"I'm going to his room. I'll come back before morning," she says.

"Are you sure he's okay?" I ask her.

She smiles brightly. "Don't worry, Zoë. I can take care of myself."

We part there, and I head up to my room and Google "fire in Ottawa" and refine my search to the past six months. There are seventeen, ranging from backyard leaf burning to the arson of an entire apartment block. I scan them all, trying to see if I can glimpse anyone who resembles Larry, but find nothing. One of the stories is particularly chilling: a house fire in which a woman and her two children died. There is no mention of arson or crime. The woman was divorced, and her ex-husband was overseas when it happened. "A terrible accident," the news report says, but I can't help thinking about Larry. He is of the right age.

Kari slips into our room at 5:08 a.m. She opens the bar fridge and sticks something in it. Then she undresses quietly and gets into bed. I wonder what she put in there. A water bottle? A drink? Probably something she's planning to use in one of her installations. Since returning from Hong Kong, Kari has re-invented herself as a "reclaimed artist," I'm not kidding, that's what she calls herself. I've been teasing her that the re-claiming is the junk she uses, and that "the reclaimed junk artist," would be more fitting, especially without the hyphen. She laughs, and tells me that she's getting rich, junk artist or not, while I'm struggling with my editing jobs in a world that doesn't want to be edited.

I listen to her breathing, trying to decide whether or not to mention my Google search. "Kari?" I whisper finally. "Are you still awake?"

"Yeah," she says. "What's up?"

I turn over so that we are facing each other in the dark. On the night table between us, the green digits of the clock radio radiate an eerie unearthly light over Kari's face. *Lime*light.

"Are you sure about this guy?" I say.

"There are no sure things, Zoë," Kari says, in her disparaging tone of voice.

"You know what I mean," I say, and then I tell her about the Google search. What if he burned down his house with his wife and kids in it? Why can't she for once just choose an ordinary man who is no threat to anyone, including herself?

"You're making stuff up," Kari says. "Larry is a perfectly sweet guy who happens to have had some trauma, and now he's trying to remember himself. Why do you have to make him a murderer?"

I raise myself up on one elbow. "What if the trauma were a murder? I mean, how do you know?" I drop onto my back and stare at the ceiling. I can just make out in the early morning light.

We are both quiet for a bit. Then Kari says, "I took the condom."

"What?" I sit right up now.

"DNA," she says. "I know someone at the university who can send it out, or whatever you're supposed to do with it."

"Does he know?" I ask, though I'm sure he doesn't.

"Don't be ridiculous," she says. "If he knew, I wouldn't have to take the damn condom."

I lie back down and think about this. So Kari, too, is not all that sure of him. She chooses these strange men because she likes the possibility of danger.

"And I know about that fire," she says. "I looked it up too,"

I sigh. "He's not going to hang out with us, is he? I mean, this is supposed to be a family trip."

"Remember the last time we were here, and you thought you kept seeing Lawrence around every corner?" She laughs, and I do recall, because it was early in our relationship, when Lawrence still made me believe that he was going to leave his wife and we were going to live happily ever after. And now twelve years have passed and he's still married, and I'm still here. Waiting.

"And his name is Larry," Kari says in her animated voice, "because I gave it to him. Because it's your lover's name. I thought we should both have dead-end lovers named Lawrence."

I want to sit up and argue with her, but I know I'd lose. "Dead-end is better than murderer," I say, then turn towards the wall, and pull the pillow over my head.

Knock, knock. "Girls?" Knock, knock. "Girls? Are you awake?" Knock, knock, knock. Mom's voice. "It's seven-thirty. You don't want to miss breakfast."

Dad's voice to Mom: "Let them miss breakfast if they want."

"We're up," I lie. "We'll see you on the patio."

Kari rolls over and opens a slit of an eye. Groans. "Fuck," she says and rolls back onto her stomach.

I get up slowly. I have a massive headache, not because I drank a lot, but because I didn't get enough sleep. If I feel this bad, I can't imagine how Kari feels. I dig around in my cosmetics case for Tylenol. Take a couple. "Want some Tylenol?" I say.

Kari groans again, which I take to mean "yes," because she stirs and lifts herself on one elbow. I pass her the water and pills.

After this, we both lie in bed a bit longer, then get up slowly, shower and dress in silence. By the time we get out to the patio, we're almost feeling normal, and neither of us has mentioned last night.

Seated at the table with Mom and Dad is a couple — psychologists, both of them — who Mom befriended between seven-thirty and now. Kari and I drink coffee and say little. I'm fascinated by the psychologists' use of very careful language, meant not to invalidate. Everything, everyone they treat with equal consideration — the trivial and mundane elevated; the interesting and important diminished.

"Excuse me," Kari says, and gets up. "I forgot something in my room."

Mom smiles at her.

I wonder if she really has forgotten something, or if she is going to call Larry, or Tom. I wish I knew more about Kari, but she has always been an enigma, sometimes friendly, sometimes hostile.

"I'm going to brush my teeth," I say, and get up too. However, in the washroom, I take out my cell and text:

*Me:* I miss you.

Nothing for three minutes.

*Lawrence:* I'm in the middle of a class.

*Me:* How about you fly down and join me?

*Lawrence:* Let's not do this again. We'll talk when you get back.

He might as well have said Over and Out. The finality of his words, the tone. *Let's not do this again.* I should have said that. Kari is right. Dead end.

When the magazine folded five years ago, I decided to leave Calgary, with its nasty cold winters and its oil tycoons. I can freelance edit from anywhere, but Lawrence is not about to move, and how pathetic is it that I'm stuck in a long-distance relationship with a married man who is going to remain married his entire life, and not to me. Makes me want to feign amnesia, go to his house and tell his wife I found his name in my cell, his love texts spanning years of unfulfilled promises.

I go back to breakfast, and soon Kari returns with a manila envelope. "Got it at the desk," she says, and smiles at us all. "Business. I need to wait for a courier." She heads back to the front desk.

I raise my eyebrows at her, and she shrugs, but when she's back, she whispers, "DNA sample."

After breakfast, we pack all our things into the van and head out for Dead Horse Point.

"Nasty name for a tourist attraction," Kari says.

"Maybe it's some guy's last name," I say.

"Yeah," Kari says, "like Joe Dead Horse."

Mom laughs. Dad shakes his head and starts rooting through his guidebooks for facts. Kari is driving and today, the third day of our trip, we are like children who want a change of scenery. The road is deserted; in twenty minutes, we see only one car. It is 110 degrees, not exactly prime sightseeing weather. But we have air conditioning and water and a brand new rental van, and we're all happy.

I have my own amnesia about the last time we were here, about most of our lives. Larry fears fire; I fear the glimpses of Kari's suicide attempts, the silence necessary to maintain our delicate balance. The last time we were here, Kari hurled herself into the Colorado River, and together with search and rescue personnel, she emerged like a goddess, wet and triumphant with rebirth. I shake these memories out of my head.

As we drive into Dead Horse Point State Park, we look for the natural corral described in the guidebooks. At first, it appears we are on flat land. But soon, deep canyons spring up at either side, and we realize we're travelling on top of a mesa toward a viewpoint hundreds of feet above Canyonlands. Suddenly, the canyons carve into the earth beside us. The road is an isthmus. Sheer drop-offs on either side. At its narrowest, twenty feet or so, we can see the remains of an old fence. Legend has it that in the 1800s, men would herd wild mustangs across this narrow, into the natural corral. They would then close the gate and choose the best horses for themselves. Some say the men locked the weak ones in and left them to die of thirst, in view of the Colorado river below. Others say the horses couldn't find their way off the corral and died because of their own stupidity. But I think the first version makes more sense — I can more easily believe in man's cruelty than in horses' stupidity.

We get out at the end and look at the spectacular panorama of 2000-foot canyons stretching into the horizon. Hues and delicate shades and shapes superimposed, like a silkscreen.

The canyon floor is uneven, treacherous, ledges everywhere. There are two busloads of tourists here in the middle of nowhere, who are all chattering too loudly, in a way that feels almost sacrilegious.

"Oh look," Kari says, her voice melancholic. "The dead horse."

Below us, on a flat ledge, we see the outline of a giant horse on its side.

"It's just mineral deposits," Dad says. "An accident of nature."

Mirage, I think. "You could go crazy," I say, "dying of thirst, while you can see the water."

Kari turns to me and watches me for a moment. I feel as if she is staring right through my clothes, my skin, into another part of me only she can access.

After Dead Horse Point, we continue into Canyonlands. This section is appropriately named Island in the Sky. We drive to the end, then leave Mom and Dad to rest while we follow a trail a mile and a half to the most spectacular viewpoint so far: as vast or greater than the Grand Canyon, but only 2000 feet deep. It is late afternoon, and already the canyon walls are turning pink and orange. Kari and I stand there, each in our own thoughts.

"It doesn't matter who he is," Kari says, as if picking up a conversation. "Larry's just another distraction. As for your Lawrence, well, he's an excuse to keep you from moving forward."

"Forward where?" I say, though I know what she means, and she's right.

She shrugs. "Wherever any of us are going. Through the motions of our lives."

Of course, we have the easy solutions: Kari should divorce Tom and move out into her own place. I should stop seeing Lawrence. The gate across the isthmus. Water everywhere.

"Hello. And where are you from?"

The voice startles us. We look up at a large rock protruding into the abyss and there lies a young man, shirt off, eating a sandwich. Spell broken, we reply and ask him where he's from. He tells us he has hiked down into the canyons, down to the Green River we can't see, down seventeen miles and back. He tells us where he's been, how long he's been there, what he saw, what he plans to see. He tells us he doesn't have a family, doesn't have a girlfriend. He tells us he loves solitude; always travels alone.

"Really?" Kari says, sarcasm dripping from every letter. "Is that why you're at the end of a public trail?"

The young man frowns, and I jab my elbow in Kari's side. "Just kidding," I say, pulling Kari away. Then when we are out of earshot, I say, "That was mean."

"He deserved it," she said. "Smug bastard. Everyone loves solitude unless they're alone."

I think we are all seeking connection, no matter how much we deny it, but I remain quiet, because this is one of those moments when Kari's wrath is a tornado touching down arbitrarily. I move out of the path of her destruction, waiting for whatever is next.

"I think one of them is ill," she says, suddenly, stopping mid-stride.

"Why would you say that?" I catch my breath, thinking how frail Dad looks.

"This trip. It seems strange in a way, doesn't it?"

"It's their anniversary," I say, lamely. "Surely we'd know if something were wrong."

"How would we know, Zoë?" she says, stressing my name. "Neither of us lives anywhere near them. We don't even live in the same province, for god's sakes!"

"You're making this up," I say, annoyed yet frightened too. I turn and begin down the trail.

"You just don't want to face reality!" she says.

I keep walking.

"You deserve your stupid dead-end Lawrence," she shouts after me, whirling to another topic.

I keep walking, thinking that if I don't say anything, I won't have anything to take back.

I reach the van first and collapse in the comfort of the air conditioning. "How are you two?" I say brightly, looking for signs of whatever Kari is intimating.

"Never better," Mom says. "Where's your sister?"

"Sulking along behind me after one of her outbursts."

"Oh dear," Mom says, "I was hoping… I mean you two have always been so close."

And now I think she has amnesia, but I say nothing, sticking to my family role.

Dad and I give each other a knowing, understanding look. Then, settled in our places, we wait for Kari.

*Mostly it is loss which teaches us
about the worth of things.*

—Arthur Schopenhauer

# ERASURES

Each morning, Clara leaves her White Rock condo overlooking Semiahmoo Bay and heads out for a run on the beach, her feet churning through sand. When the tide is out, she cheats by running on the hard wet surface, dodging tidal pools. Today, the beach is deserted but for a jogger, a woman walking her dog and the man building a sandcastle nearly a half-mile out. There are no children nearby, and Clara wonders who the man is, and what exactly he's doing.

For several days now, she has come across him building his structures halfway between the low tide line and shore. Today, she aims her run further out, to see what he's building and perhaps speak to him. As she approaches, he looks up, and she recognizes him from a newscast. He is the civil engineer who designed a highway bridge that recently collapsed, killing three people. Although lauded as brilliant, he has fallen from grace and is suddenly a pariah; everything he has accomplished so far is now being viewed through the lens of this error.

Closer now, she is startled by the man's construction: an intricate church about four feet high, a basilica, perhaps, with a nave and two side aisles with vaulted ceilings. Beside the church, a cemetery of crosses and headstones. She stops to admire it. The man looks up, his hands gloved in sand, his brow knit. She smiles and nods to him, then continues her jog, wondering whether he has someone to talk to. Surely this building in sand, this destruction cannot be healthy.

She picks up her newspaper from her condo doorstep, silently thanking the custodian who must have dropped it there. Inside, she makes coffee, dishes yoghurt and granola into a bowl, and opens the newspaper. On page 2, she is startled by the photo of her ex-husband, above which the caption reads: The 6th Homicide of the Year. Clara scans the article quickly, shaken. "…was attacked in a downtown parkade, suffering six stab wounds. As he lay dying, he called 911 on his cellphone and identified his assailant."

Why hasn't someone called her? Doesn't she have the right to be told? She picks up her phone, intending to call… who? She and Liam have not spoken since their divorce eight years ago.

She phones Liam's office number at the university and a stranger answers, "Yes, we've heard about the tragedy. The funeral is scheduled for two days from now. Here is his wife's phone number."

Clara hangs up, but she doesn't call the number. What is she to say? I'm Liam's ex-wife, who hasn't spoken to him since our divorce, since I chose to walk away? She gathers her courage and calls instead Liam's oldest daughter Daphne — a woman Clara's age, who has never accepted her.

"Why are you calling me?" Daphne says. "Haven't you done enough harm?"

Harm, Clara thinks. Perhaps the harm was their marriage in 2006 — oh, how distant that seems to her right now. Liam had been her thesis advisor for four years, and she had not had other serious boyfriends, being too focused on her studies. She had fallen under his spell, inadvertently, as an extension of the long hours they spent together discussing her work. They must both have mistaken dependency and admiration for love. He was sixteen years older than Clara, and it didn't take long for her to feel that he was lording his age over her, his experience over her ideas, his will over hers. Nonetheless, with the exception of that one passion-drenched summer that threatened to destroy them, they had managed to stay together for five years.

She was no wallflower. Plenty of men entered and exited her orbit, both during Liam's affairs, and well past them to the years after the divorce. But these men were like birds alighting for a rest on their migratory paths. They simply fluttered through her life for a while, then moved on with her blessing. Some called her heartless, and maybe they were right. She felt nothing.

"I haven't spoken to your father in years," Clara says. "Can't we let bygones be bygones?"

"Bygones!" Daphne shouts. "He *loved* you! You ruined his life! You ruined all our lives. And now, what do you want?"

Clara takes a deep breath. This is not how she remembers it. She'd like to remind Daphne that Liam remarried before the signatures on the divorce papers had dried. Instead, she says, "I'd like to pay my respects. May I come to the funeral?"

"Suit yourself," Daphne says, then suddenly starts sobbing. "What are we going to do without him?"

Clara listens quietly, unsure what to say now. She waits until Daphne stops crying, then writes down the name of the funeral parlour.

From the bookshelf in her home office, she takes the photo album of Liam and her life together and opens it. The photos accurately document the two of them at their wedding, smiling, eating dinners, hiking; they show them partying with friends, speaking at conferences, remodelling a house, gardening. She stares at the static faces, at their ordinary lives. They could be anyone. What the photos don't show are the inner moments, the struggles and tribulations of emotions. She tries to recall specific moments of tenderness or happiness, but they have all dissolved into a vague recollection of ennui, listlessness, discontent and ultimately estrangement. This is not how she characterized their relationship during her stint with a therapist in a support group right after the divorce, when Liam's absence left her bewildered and exposed. How is it possible, she thinks, to spend years with a man and recall nothing momentous? She closes the book and pours herself a glass of wine. "To you, Liam," she says, toasting him, guilty that she does not feel overwhelming grief or loss. He is someone she once knew, someone she once loved.

Yet, the finality of knowing she will never see him again, as well as her own selective amnesia, makes her anxious and restless. What is the point of it all, she thinks. The man on the beach daily builds structures in the way of the tide, as if welcoming destruction; her marriage to Liam was a construction too, as precarious as the beach man's; her own life, right now, feels to her like a footnote. She is thirty-seven years old, has had a meteoric career arc, but what has she to show for it? She teaches geophysics at the university, shepherding a flock of students through every semester, trying to infuse in them the magnificent dynamics of the earth, the physical history, the biological changes the earth has undergone and continues to undergo. She takes them on field trips so they can hold stones and feel the earth's movements from within. She delivers complex papers at conferences, and publishes them in peer-reviewed science journals. She has always thought of her career as a vocation — something important, yet in the face of mortality, it seems trivial. The earth will continue its ebbs and flows without and despite humankind. What she knows will die with her, and in a generation or two, no one will remember she even existed.

Liam's death unleashes a cache of memories, not of Liam, but of Antonio, the ideal, the *real* love she missed, the Italian student she met in her last year of graduate studies at university. Though in different faculties and departments — she in geophysics and he in history — they became fast friends, and despite the fact that she was engaged to Liam and Antonio had a casual girlfriend back home, they soon became lovers. Why hadn't she broken her engagement? She shakes her head, trying to recall her own state of mind back then. What future could she have had with Antonio? Should she have abandoned her goals and gone to live with him in Italy? Liam offered her stability and security. He could help her move forward in her career, and he did.

She showers, then chooses a grey sweater and black skirt — something funereal. She gathers her papers into her briefcase and heads to the university. In the car, she speed dials her sister Olivia in California, puts her on speaker phone so she can drive.

"Liam's dead," she says as soon as Olivia picks up.

"Whaaaat? How?"

"Murdered, apparently, by someone he knew."

"That's crazy," Olivia says. "It sounds like something you see on TV. Liam was not that kind of guy."

"As if there's a kind of guy who gets murdered," Clara says.

"Who do you think did it?" Olivia asks.

"I don't know. Haven't thought about it really." And she hadn't thought about it, startled and shocked by the news. Who would want to kill Liam?

"A colleague, maybe? Or a jealous husband, do you think?" Olivia sounds excited. "What about that lover you had years ago? Maybe he came back and did Liam in."

"You really have been watching too much TV," Clara says. "This isn't a joke."

"I know, I know. I'm sorry. It's just that Liam was so long ago." She pauses. "Are you terribly sad about it?"

"Of course I'm sad about it," Clara says, exasperated. "I'd be sad if anyone I knew was murdered suddenly."

"Well, don't obsess over it, okay? You always obsess over everything," Olivia says, as if she were continuing some other conversation.

"Listen, I'm in the car. I've got to go. We'll talk later."

Clara hangs up, frustrated with Olivia's lack of sympathy or empathy. It's just like Olivia to hurl the past at her. Antonio. She sighs, and her eyes well up unexpectedly.

They used to meet, she and Antonio, in secluded areas — darkened theatres, park trails, rented cars — hideaways which heightened their passion. Antonio teased her, likening their hiding to people from his region of Italy — the Marche — who, during times of war, retreated to the safety of numerous refuges — both natural caves and man-made ones — sculpted with hammers and chisels into the cliffs and mountainsides. Some were ancient Etruscan and Roman drainage channels still in use, he told her, unlike anything you'd find in Canada. Others were caverns sculpted by water dripping through stone — natural shelters for animals at night, for cold storage, for the processing of milk and cheese, for safety. When you come to Fossombrone, he said, we'll go and explore them. His animation and enthusiasm were infectious. The magic of water carving stone, gnawing a rocky base into dwellings for people and animals and organisms; the magic that these caves could remain hidden for hundreds, thousands, millions of years, then suddenly be found.

She hadn't meant to go, and had a suitcase of reasons why not: it wasn't right, she'd lost her head, she was engaged, he was a distraction, she had to concentrate, etc. However, as the days and weeks after Antonio's departure grew, so did her craving for him, overcoming her guilt. She told Liam she wanted a break on her own before the wedding, and booked a flight to Italy.

Liam was hesitant, but didn't try to dissuade her. However, two days before she left, he brought home an envelope with an offer for her: a sessional teaching appointment at the university in the fall.

After a microwaved supper that evening, she texts her friend Zoë to meet her for a drink at the local bar; tells her about Liam.

"Liam was a jerk," Zoë says.

"Don't say that. He's dead." This is not the first time Zoë has expressed these thoughts. She often said it while Clara was married.

"Doesn't make him less of a jerk," Zoë says.

"Still…"

"Still nothing. So he's dead. Have you forgotten the cheating?" She shakes her head.

"Did you ever sleep with Liam?" Clara says suddenly. She leans forward a little, and when Zoë hesitates, she adds, "I don't care if you did," she says. "Not any more. Not now."

"Nah," Zoë says, but she doesn't meet Clara's eyes. "Besides, · my big affair has always been Lawrence."

"Long distance non-affair, you mean," Clara says. "Did you ever think of Lawrence's wife? And don't say that's different."

Zoë sighs. "I know. I know. You're right. The cheating's probably what keeps the marriage together." She laughs. "I guess I'm the glue."

"Didn't work too well for me," Clara says, wondering at what point the cheating began, or whether he always had lovers, and at what point her indifference began. "Even so, I owe Liam a lot," she adds, thinking of the strings he must have pulled to help her career along.

"That's what he wanted you to think," Zoë says. "So you would always be grateful, and he could do what he wanted."

Clara shrugs. She tries to remember herself with Liam those early years. She was so unsure of herself. She'd idolized him. "He had…connections," she says.

"Connections/ shmections," Zoë says. "You're terrific at what you do. You don't really think you would have gotten tenure if you weren't?" She shakes her head. "You don't owe him a thing."

Clara is not totally convinced. "Liam was the level-headed one. I was too impulsive. He evened me out."

"Flattened you out, is more like it," Zoë says.

She'd acted on impulse that summer, and Liam had secured her a job, had secured her return.

Antonio had met her at the airport in Rome, his eyes shiny with happiness, his arms wrapping her to him, his lips pressing against hers until she was breathless. They took two trains and a bus to arrive in Fossombrone, and on the way he told her he'd had an interview at the University of Urbino and been offered a job in the fall. His parents' house was large enough for now; he would commute, it wasn't far. Then later…there were plenty of houses for rent. She didn't tell him about the sessional appointment back home.

He had booked her into a B & B a couple of blocks from the central plaza and bus station, though he had wanted her to stay at his family home. Clara had declined, feeling the pressure too great. She worried even meeting his parents would imply a promise she was not ready to make. They had discussed it back in Canada, this long-distance relationship that threatened to pull everyone apart.

"Many couples commute," Antonio said.

"Maybe across the country," Clara said. "Not across the Atlantic." She paused. "We'd see each other once a year. That's not a relationship."

"Penelope waited twenty," he said, mock-pouting, and Clara laughed.

The Fossombrone B & B was a house rebuilt in the 1950s, as many were after the German bombardment of WWII. Antonio was nervous, relating historical facts, like a tour guide. The furniture dated to the 1800s and was rescued from the rubble by the father of the current proprietor, he said, and Clara thought about fossils, preserved, arrested in time, and hidden until exposed little by little by determined paleontologists. She imagined the skeletons of chairs and tables and armoires half-buried in the detritus of war, waiting to be discovered.

In her room at the B & B, as soon as the owner left them, they shut the door, undressed hastily and made love.

"I am so happy you're finally here," he said afterwards, leaning on one elbow to look at her. "My parents will like you."

"Do I have to meet them today?" she asked, teasing.

"Later. For dinner. Right now, I want to show you around."

They dressed and wandered out to the central square, from which the town rose up the hill of Sant'Aldebrando, terraced in various strata, like the earth itself. Above the town were the ruins of the Malatesta Fortress, strategically built in the middle of the Metauro valley, in order to control the Via Flaminia. She knew all about the ancient Roman road over the

Apennines between Rome and Rimini, still in use after 2000 years. She wondered what would be left behind from modern civilization.

"You're lucky," she told Antonio. "You're rooted here, through generations. Canada is too young a nation."

"You suffer from a poverty of history," he said.

"We have petroglyphs," Clara said, "but because they tend to be intertidal carvings, they've been badly eroded. Few can even be dated. But they are evidence that humans lived there hundreds, maybe thousands of years ago." In Canada nowadays, she thought, everything is disposable, used and discarded, replaced with the new.

"You can come and live here," Antonio said. "You can share our history."

She didn't respond, and he took her hand and led her along the porticoed main street, then up small picturesque pathways connecting the various levels, often no more than four feet across, with rows of stones at wide intervals to keep one from slipping. For a moment, she wondered if she could live here, with Antonio. She could start over, learn Italian, maybe get hired as an English instructor, her imagined life zigzagging ahead of her, just as they were doing now physically up to the top of the hill, where they looked down over a vast panorama through which snaked the Metauro river.

"That's our house down there," Antonio said, pointing to the left.

Clara wasn't sure which house he meant, but it didn't matter. She'd see it soon enough.

"It would become ours one day," he said.

She sighed, and they began their descent, bearing right. A black cat skittered in front of them, and Antonio made the sign of the cross. Clara laughed. "Seriously?" she said.

He smiled. "Habit."

Down below, at the level of the highway, loomed the ancient Roman single-arch bridge she'd seen in photos. In the late afternoon light, the bridge was reflected in the water so as to become a circle. An elusive eternity symbol. Things, Clara thought, are rarely what they seem. Antonio's hand rested in the small of her back, circled her waist, held her hand. What was she getting into? She had spent her entire adult life studying. She had promised herself to Liam. Yet Antonio was her first and only love. She was twenty-four, with seemingly unlimited opportunities ahead of her.

The following day, Antonio drove her to Gola del Furlo, to show her Italy's "Grand Canyon."

"They hated me," Clara said.

"No, you're wrong." Antonio stroked her inner arm.

He parked the car in the gravel beside the entrance to the Roman tunnel, and they walked along the emerald river, which though unthreatening now, had carved this gorge at the narrowest point between Pietralata and Paganuccio mountains. Gola del Furlo, the Throat of the Furlo. Clara imagined a giant floating on its waters, the gorge at its throat.

"I couldn't even speak to them," she said. "How could they get to know me if we can't communicate?" She didn't know any Italian, and although both Antonio's parents had smiled, his mother's eyes had remained cold. Antonio had explained about his girlfriend Licia, who was not really his girlfriend, he said, because their parents were lifelong friends, and *they* had expected the marriage. He liked the young woman, they had dated on and off for several years, but he had never promised anything more.

Clara wasn't sure whether this was meant to appease her, or whether it was true.

They stood for a few moments staring at the water, then at the inscription above the tunnel. Clara read the English plaque. Furlo Pass, it read, omitting the marvellous image of the throat, which perhaps was too dramatic for the English sensibility.

"Anyway, it doesn't matter what they think," Antonio said, taking her hand and leading her along the highway to where Passo Del Furlo culminated in several buildings. They stopped in front of The Bar Furlo and Hotel Antico Furlo, which,

Antonio told her, had a bedroom preserved as it was when Mussolini stayed there with a lover.

"Why would they want to remember that nasty bit of history?" Clara said.

"Nasty or not, it's still history," Antonio said, frowning. "How can we learn from the mistakes of the past if we pretend they never existed?"

Clara smiled. "Are you suggesting we should preserve the Trump hotels for all eternity?"

"Maybe it's okay to erase him," Antonio said, and laughed.

"*Venite. Venite.* Come," a soft voice called out to them.

They turned and saw a small wiry man, seventy or so, waving as if he knew them. Spread out in front of him were two long tables filled with stones. "This museum is open," he said.

Clara beamed.

"I knew you'd like this," Antonio said.

Clara squeezed his hand, grateful for his thoughtfulness, his trying to please her.

On the tables were hundreds of fossils and stones.

"I've been collecting these for thirty-one years," the man said. "I've dug them out of mines and quarries, I've climbed up mountains, I've found them near the riverbed. Not only me, but my friends too." He spoke quickly, his voice excited, and Antonio translated.

Clara turned the specimens over in her hands, marvelling at the delicate crystal ammonites embedded in the stones, fossils 200 million years old.

"Magnificent," she murmured.

"Would you like to see more?" the man asked. "I have many more inside."

They followed him into the house. Every flat surface was covered with fossils and stones: the chairs, the tables, the stools, the commodes. How did he live a normal life here, Clara wondered. Did he move stones when he needed to sit down? Was his bed made of stones, or of crystallized ammonites, like an exquisite carved piece of art? They examined each rock and the man named them, explained where he'd found them. She knew this area was one of the richest and most famous ammonite deposits in Europe.

"I have something special in the basement," the man said. "Follow me."

Antonio took her hand and they stepped down into a dank, humid room. The man had excavated a circular grotto in the basement, like a miniature apse, inside of which were hundreds of stones placed all around in niches and layers. In front of the grotto was a locked iron gate.

"Stand there," the man said, and turned out the lights. For a moment, they were plunged into darkness, and Clara wondered what they'd gotten themselves into. Then the man flicked a switch, and a black light shone in the grotto, turning the stones into the most spectacular iridescent greens, reds, oranges, purples, blues. They looked as if they had been painted by hand.

"They're fluorescent stones," the man said, "common enough here, if you know where to look." Clara stood transfixed, imagining a whole mountainside glowing, thinking about the hidden mineral depths of the earth.

On her last night in Italy, Antonio gave her a gold pendant with a sliced ammonite embedded in white stone. She recognized it immediately as a crystallized ammonite like the ones in the rock museum. He placed the chain around her neck so the translucent ribs of the ammonite lay just past her collarbones. And after supper, when they stood outside in the evening dark, he surprised her with a special UV flashlight he aimed at the delicate bones of the ammonite, which shimmered on her chest.

She goes to the funeral with Zoë, and they sit at the back, where they will not be conspicuous. Having a church service seems odd, given that Liam was not religious; was, in fact, quite outspoken against organized religion. Perhaps he changed when he met his third wife. Everyone stands for the funeral cortège: first the coffin, followed by his current wife — an ex-student, the last of Liam's affairs while he and Clara were married — then two small children, then Daphne. Clara glances around, wondering which of the older women sitting with Daphne is the first wife. We might all three be here, she thinks, three generations of women, three separate compartments, who know nothing of each other's lives. A poverty of history.

Zoë stares at her phone, thumb-typing until they are all seated once more. Then she nudges Clara, pointing to the screen. Disgruntled student arrested.... Clara takes the phone and reads, while the minister begins the service. One by one, people stand and give testimony to Liam's life and person in obvious clichés: *he was kind*...She half-listens, thinking that it's so anticlimactic — a student unhappy with a failing grade — *generous, funny, smart...* thinking it impossible that one could die over a failing grade, yet she has seen those true crime stories on the Investigation Discovery Channel, in which hour after hour people commit heinous crimes for the most banal reasons — *a good husband, a good father, a good employee, a good fill-in-the-blanks*. It is both strange and familiar to Clara. Liam's achievements have been reduced to buzzwords, his life turned into a boilerplate of goodwill.

She frowns. Is this really what he was to everyone? To her? She has come to think of him as an impediment, an obstacle to her happiness, though she knows this is not true. Perhaps once he was, but even this seems too easy an accusation. Her inaction is her own doing. She *chose* Liam. She *chose* career. Ultimately, she chose silence. Why did she not go back to Italy right after her divorce? Was she embarrassed? Afraid to break the spell of the perfect love? Fearful Antonio might reject her?

She is still frowning when everyone files out of the church. Daphne looks through her.

Two weeks after the funeral, she flies to Rome, a return journey, retracing her steps, the two trains, the bus.

Then she is in Fossombrone, in a rented car, checked into the same hotel, into the same room she occupied thirteen years ago. The owner's daughter is friendly, speaks English, and when Clara asks if she knows Antonio's family name, the young woman nods. "It's a small town," she says. "Less than 10,000 people." She takes out her phone and in a few clicks has Antonio's parents' phone number.

The young woman calls the number, asks for Antonio, then shakes her head. "He's at work," she says, "and will be back later today. Is there a phone number I can leave?"

Clara leaves her name and cell number, then walks out into the town, a memory replay up and down the cobblestone streets.

In late afternoon, she heads out along Via Flaminia to the tunnel, the Furlo Antico hotel. She parks the car in the restaurant lot, wondering if Antonio is married, if he will remember her.

She is in front of the hotel when a tall, blonde woman approaches from the Bar Furlo. As she walks, she quickly unties her white server's apron, exposing a pale blue sweater over tan pants. "I'm sorry," she says, "the hotel is closed for the season."

Across the street from the hotel is a large IN VENDITA sign. FOR SALE.

"The hotel and restaurant are closed today, but the bar serves food." She points to the adjacent building. "If you come back tomorrow, I'll show you Mussolini's room."

Clara shakes her head. "*Grazie*, no." She shudders at the thought.

The woman hands her a fan of postcards depicting Mussolini's bedroom and the dining room where Mussolini ate, preserved with the furniture of the era Mussolini had shipped from Rome.

"Il Duce stayed here fifty-six times with his lover Clara Petacci," the woman says. "They were on their way to Predappio from Rome. Claretta, they called her." She has launched into her tourist spiel. "And look up there," she says. "Made in 1936."

Clara shudders, hearing her name in this new context, recalling that Mussolini and Claretta were executed by firing squad, thrown in Milan's Piazzale Loreto along with other executed fascists so that people could beat, kick, shoot, urinate and spit on their corpses, then they were hanged upside down on meat hooks, from the metal girders of a service station. She hands back the postcards and follows the woman's gaze. She can barely make out the Mussolini profile blasted into the slopes of Mount Pietralata. Fortunately, during WWII, resistance fighters bombed its nose off, and now a forest has almost completely covered its features. If she hadn't been told, she would not have known it had ever existed.

She turns back to the FOR SALE sign. "Signora," she says, pointing, "didn't a man live there who collected rocks?"

The woman nods. "He died," she says. "Three years ago."

"And the rocks?"

The woman shrugs. "Some were given away, some went to a museum in Milan. There's still a small museum in the basement. Do you care to see it?"

"Please," Clara says. She follows the woman across the street, conjuring the ghost of the old man. The yard is overgrown, the place deserted.

"You have one of our stones," the woman says now, motioning Clara to the side of the building.

Clara nods, and fingers the ammonite at her neck. It is as beautiful as it was all those years ago. She recalls reading that in ancient times, ammonites were believed to be a gift from the stars, and that their connection to the past encouraged the recall of memory. Liam is dead, she thinks, and it's Liam I betrayed, Liam I married but didn't love, Liam who betrayed me. Yet all I want is to return to the intensity of longing, to return to that last night with Antonio, to change the past.

She follows the woman down a flight of outside stairs. The woman unlocks the door, leads her into a small room that contains three glass showcases of rocks embedded with ammonites, and the grotto in its entirety, with the fluorescent stones. The woman turns on the black light, but without full darkness, the effect is ruined: the stones ordinary, their colours faded. For a fleeting moment, Clara sees herself and Antonio

127

captivated by the small miracle of the stones exposed, while she resisted, and kept her secrets hidden.

"Is the house for sale?" Clara asks.

"It's been for sale for two years," the woman says. She shakes her head.

"What will happen to the museum?"

"When it sells, the museum will go, I suppose." She turns out the black light, and begins to walk towards the door.

"But shouldn't it all be kept? It's his life's work," Clara says.

The woman shrugs.

"What about the man who collected all this?" Clara asks. "What can you tell me about him?"

The woman looks at her suspiciously. She shrugs again. "Nothing really. He collected stones."

Clara would like to tell her that in Roman times, legacy was prized more than life itself. And the greatest insult was to erase one's lifetime's accomplishments from the annals of history, as if they had never existed. *Damnatio memoriae*, the damnation of memory.

They walk back to the Bar Furlo, where Clara eats supper, until her cell rings and his voice reaches across the years. "Clara."

"Antonio?" she says. "I didn't know...." She pauses. "I was passing through...I thought I'd say hello." Her heart is beating so hard, she is sure he can hear it.

"Where are you?" he says, as if they had spoken yesterday, the years melted away.

She buys a box full of rocks, rare fluorescent ones, inside which nestle ammonites—delicate and translucent. She wants to recreate the grotto, to remember. The stones have magic properties: they convey the sound of the Candigliano River, reflect the carved walls of the Furlo tunnel, glow with yearning for The Marche and that lonely switchback road eight kilometres up Mount Pietralata, to the head of a trail leading to a panoramic viewpoint directly below the chin of Mussolini, where the two of them had sat in his black borrowed car, windows rolled down.

"I only want to be with you," he said.

An SUV had pulled up right then, startling them, and parked. Antonio's declaration had echoed in the air between them, suspended, while three women and a man emerged from the van and walked past them up the trail to the lookout. Clara had been to that stone balcony with Antonio days before, had stared at the vastness of the Appenines, the Furlo canyon, the Adriatic Sea, feeling small and insignificant.

"It's impossible," Clara had said. She thought about the sessional job awaiting her in Vancouver. She thought about all the years she spent studying. She had worked too hard to quit now. "I can't just abandon my life and stay here."

"What about love?" he said, and she remained silent, listening to Ann Wilson's voice in her head, singing *What about love? Don't you want someone to care about you?*…

Clara waits at the edge of Via Flaminia, the ancient Roman road, staring at the seafoam green of the Candigliano river at Gola del Furlo, trying to imagine its force and fury before it was dammed almost 100 years ago, trying to remember the tempest of her own emotions. She thinks of the man who collected stones, of her and Antonio's breathless love, of Liam's death, of her own loneliness. How little they matter in geological time. She fingers the stone around her neck, lifts it and stares at the ammonite trapped inside it, a memory 140 million years old. In a tree above her, jackdaws chatter, and the river continues its flow.

*Remembrance of things past is not necessarily
the remembrance of things as they were.*

— Marcel Proust

# STRAYS

They'd trekked out in early afternoon, and here they still are, at almost 6:30, the sun already receded into the horizon, the sky a darkening hue, and the two of them no further in their mission. A cacophony rises from nearby marshes: the stridor of crickets, the trills and jackhammers of bullfrogs, the high-pitched squeals of Great White Egrets as they circle and glide, then swoop behind the treed skyline. Denise stops a moment to watch them, wondering what's drawing them all to that particular location.

Guy stops too, a little impatiently. "Now what?" he says.

She points.

"They're just going to roost," he says, dismissing her. "We should get back before dark." He resumes walking.

She knows he considers this wandering up and down streets a colossal waste of time. They've crossed rice fields, rivulets and irrigation ditches. Yet the ramshackle restaurants, the caravan resorts, the Royal temple, the stuccoed prangs, the courtyards, and the markets have not yielded anything. Does she really believe they're going to stumble into her father? Or is she expecting him to walk out of one of the houses, arms open? They're both hot and thirsty. In three days, Guy is flying back to the US, and this is making them both — for different reasons — anxious and sulky.

She shrugs and follows him along a narrow road between corrugated rooftops, rickety stilt-shacks, and guest houses parallel to the ocean. Her father might be ensconced in one of them. They've passed one public beach and two tiny convenience stores selling potato chips, insect repellent, thumb drives, water, ice cream — fare meant for tourists and travellers. Up ahead, three old and sickly stray dogs litter the road. Seven more — mangy and malnourished, grizzled, and injured, most with scaly bald patches — lie in the shadows of dusk, barely raising their heads when Denise and Guy walk past.

"They're so sad," Denise says. "Poor things." She stops, raises the camera strapped around her neck, unscrews the lens cover, and takes a few shots. Though she's been in Thailand three weeks, she is still disconcerted by the packs of dogs that roam the streets — a handful of the 8.5 million in the country, of which almost a million are dogs abandoned by their owners. She wonders how people can be so cruel, especially people who are Buddhists. Aren't they supposed to not even harm flies? Clichés, she thinks. Human beings are capable of incredible cruelty no matter what their religion.

Guy continues walking, apparently unmoved by the ailing dogs scattered around them. Denise wants to gather them all and nurse them back to health. How have these sick, old creatures come together? Have they been chased out of other packs, or been abandoned, or have they left on their own when confronted with younger, stronger dogs? She thinks of retirement homes, of assisted-living facilities, an entire industry revolving around the concealment of the infirm and the elderly. She thinks of her mother at home, alone, languishing in her city condo.

"We have to do something!" she says, surprising herself with the ferocity of her voice.

"Like what?" Guy turns to her.

"I was talking about my dad," Denise says.

"What do you want to do?" Guy stops in the middle of the road and faces her.

She stops too. "I have to…find him. I have to bring him home."

He sighs. "Maybe he doesn't want to be found." He turns and continues walking towards their hotel.

A year ago, her parents went on holiday to Thailand, and inexplicably — because she refused to talk about it — only her mother returned. Denise was certain it was all a terrible mistake, an impulsive decision possibly fuelled by alcohol. A month passed, two, then four, eight, and all the while, her father sent postcards of beaches and monuments, as if he were on holiday and would return soon. The last postcard her mother received over four months ago depicted a stunning Thai girl with orchids in her hair against a tropical garden. On the back, her father had written, "Life is wonderful." When her mother showed her the postcard, Denise rolled her eyes, and her mother said, "Good for you, asshole!" while Denise patted her back in sympathy. So Dad was having a good time. What did that make their lives? She thinks about that postcard now, and suddenly, his words seem loaded with meaning. Was he comparing his new life to his old one? Was he wishing them all to get on with their own lives? And why couldn't he, like the rest of the world, get an email address?

Her worry turned to alarm a month ago, when her mother was served the divorce papers, and soon after, her father abruptly withdrew half the funds from their joint savings account. Denise scoured the web and found disturbing stories of extortions, disappearances, and gang-style executions. She began to invent terrible scenarios of kidnapping and ransom and murder. She phoned her brothers, Travis in Montreal and Robbie in Toronto. Both dismissed her fears, with varying degrees of skepticism. "He always comes back," Robbie said. Perhaps her anxiety mushroomed because she had returned to live with her mother — temporarily — and her father's absence loomed large between them. Perhaps she preferred apocalyptic scenarios to the belief that her father would completely abandon his former life, as if his wife and children no longer existed.

She asked for a leave of absence from her work as a health care administrator, and told her depressed and melancholy mother that she was going to a conference, not wanting to present her with hope. What if her father was unreachable, either physically or emotionally? And why didn't her mother remember all the unpleasantness, the neglect, the ennui? It was as if she were suffering from voluntary amnesia. A part of Denise is disgusted with her mother also.

"He's an asshole," Travis says now, when she calls him from her hotel room in Thailand. "He's doing what he always does."

"This feels different," Denise says. "The money, the divorce papers."

"So maybe it's about time," Travis says. "Mom should have left him years ago."

He's probably right, Denise thinks. If she were to open the illustrated storybook of her life, she'd find her father's lapses during his forty years of wedded misery. And if her storybook had sound, she'd hear the repetitive circular arguments, the silence, her mother's muffled sobs. How many stupid affairs could a husband have and still be married to the same woman? Denise had imagined that once she and her brothers were out of the house, her father would change, settle into his life. *Stop it!* she tells herself now.

"Maybe he needs to find himself," her younger brother Robbie says. "I think he's fundamentally unhappy."

"Maybe," Denise says, wondering why Robbie always excuses their father's behaviour. Finding himself, indeed. Why couldn't her father do what other men do: buy a red sports car, take up hockey, grow a ponytail — any of a dozen clichés to staunch a mid- or in his case two-third-life crisis. More likely, he's massaging his ego with a nubile Thai girl, who might be poor and supporting an extended family. A fair trade. After all, it wasn't so long ago that well-bred English girls without fortunes were expected to marry money, without expectation of romance or personal fulfilment. (She's been reading Anthony Trollope, in whose books penniless young women "teach themselves" to love appropriate wealthy men.) She doesn't blame whoever the Thai girl is, but she is totally disgusted with her father, embarrassed by his angst, appalled by his vanity. Why can't he teach himself to love his wife?

Doesn't his family mean anything to him? How can he be so callous and so selfish?

Before she came to Thailand, when it was clear that her father was no longer returning home, Denise had gone in search of his best friend Norman, an accountant in his firm, so socially awkward, they all felt sorry for him. When Norman's mother died, he'd received a large insurance settlement with which he'd purchased a mansion in one of the most exclusive neighbourhoods in Vancouver. Then he went to Thailand for a holiday and returned a month later with a Thai wife thirty-some years younger than himself, a girl he paraded from house to house, as if Lawan were a trophy he'd won in an Olympic competition. Over six years, they had had two children. The few times Denise had visited with her father, she had been embarrassed by the man's heavy use of taxidermy in his décor: the giant stuffed eagle above the entrance, the deer heads in the lobby, squirrels and beavers atop the wainscotting, and the bearskin rug in front of the fireplace, complete with bear claws, as if the bear had been skinned alive.

He answered her repeated ringing of the doorbell, unshaven, uncombed, his eyes rimmed in red and bloodshot, as though he'd been on a bender, though this seemed out of character. She peered around him, trying to see Lawan and the children.

"They're gone," Norman said, with such finality that Denise knew he meant something serious.

"Gone?" she said. "Gone where?"

"Vamoose. She's got a lawyer. Took the kids," he said, his voice breaking. He stepped aside. "Do you want to come in?"

Denise hesitated. Norman stared at her expectantly. She didn't want to enter that dark lobby, that house where dead creatures were displayed dispassionately, but she felt pity for the man. Besides, she wanted to ask him about her father.

As soon as she crossed the threshold, Norman's hand touched the small of her back, and she stepped forward as if an Australian cattle dog had nipped at her heels. In the living room, she let him lead her to the couch.

"I gave her everything," he said, sitting beside her. "This house. Clothes. Toys for the kids. Jewellery. Anything she wanted she could have. And what does she do? She runs away." He violently slapped the seat cushion, and Denise recoiled, feeling as if she'd found herself in the midst of a cyclone, with no idea how she got there. The times she'd seen Lawan and Norman together, they'd appeared happy. However, who was to say what went on inside a couple's private life? She murmured sympathetic sounds, though she wanted to say, my father's gone too.

"And now," Norman said, standing up and pacing in front of her, "she's told the lawyer a bunch of lies — about me abusing the children — I LOVE those children!" He stamped his foot.

Denise didn't know what to say now, her sympathies dwindling. She shrugged. "Of course you do."

"She wants half the house!" he said. "This house was bought with my mother's money!" He continued to pace, agitated, and Denise squirmed. "I'm going to lose everything!"

She took a deep breath, trying to think of something to calm him. He looked wild to her now. She shouldn't have come into the house. "I'm sure it will all work out," she said, vaguely. "These things do. I'm sorry — "

"You know what I should have done?" He stopped in front of her, and leaned in, eye-to-eye.

She shook her head.

"I should have killed her, that's what. Then I would have gone to jail for a few years — crime of passion — and I would still have my house." He crossed his arms and stared at her.

She could see he was dead serious. "I'm sure you don't really mean that," she said, uttering a small nervous laugh.

He continued to stare at her for a moment, then he sank into an armchair, his head in his hands, his shoulders shaking with silent sobs.

She stood up, and took a few steps towards the door. "I...I really need to get going. Is there someone I can call?"

He shook his head without looking up.

"Take care," she said, padding through the lobby to the front door.

"And I did mean it!" he yelled after her.

She walked slowly back to her car, then quickly locked the doors. Could it be possible that shy, pathetic Norman was an abuser? Or had he been taken in by the woman's flattery and youth? She didn't know what to believe. How quickly one could fall from grace.

She drove home, no closer to finding out where her father might have gone.

"He must be around here somewhere," Guy says now, as they continue to tramp through the dusty streets. "We just need to find expats. Someone will know him. Thailand is famous for retirees looking for sun, low cost of living. And then there's the girls —"

"Stop it!" Denise says. "You are all disgusting." She marches on past him, but he catches up, takes her arm, leans in close and kisses her.

She doesn't know Guy, not really. He's twenty-eight — four years younger than she is, an engineer, tall, grey-eyed, physically her type. She met him in Bangkok a few days after she arrived. Both were staying at the same hotel. Guy was on a holiday with a group of men he ditched soon after he met Denise. She was on a mission, and he was happy to tag along. They've told each other abridged versions of their pasts — she of her philandering father, therapists, ex-live-in lover, an abandoned mother, a rescue dog and two cats; he of his divorced parents, sometime girlfriend, a stepsister, two dogs and a cat. They bonded over their animals, sharing photos, and soon after, a hotel room.

With Guy, following her father's tracks felt as if they were playing a mystery board game — Bounty Hunters in Bangkok, though she was determined to take her father home with her. They went to the address in the divorce papers and found a two-storey lime green guest house on a narrow unpaved street. No one remembered her father specifically, something Denise could understand, given that most of the guests were retirement-age *farangs*. How could her father have fallen to this level of pathetic? Denise pulled out a photo taken a year before, and circulated it until one of the men at the guest house thought he remembered him.

"I think he said he was headed for Chiang Mai," the man said. He was wearing knee-length tan shorts and a floppy faded-black T-shirt that read PHUKET.

"It's a big city," Denise said, imagining herself sifting through over 170,000 people. "Can you be more specific? Was he on his own?"

The man stared at her, sizing her up. He looked at Guy.

"He's my dad," Denise said.

"I don't know," the man said, now a bit reluctantly. "He might have been with someone —"

"Does this someone have a name? Surely my dad left a forwarding address?"

Finally, the man went inside, spoke to the owner in Thai, and came back out with a slip of paper, on which was written the forwarding hotel name. They thanked him and left.

"Next time," Guy said, as they walked back to their hotel, "let me handle it. You're far too hostile."

"I didn't say anything."

"It's the tone of your voice. You're judging them."

"Well, of course I'm judging them," she snapped. "Where else is it okay for retirees to be coupling with twenty-year-olds? Would they be doing this in their own countries?" She let out an exasperated sigh.

"They probably would," Guy said wryly, "if they could only get twenty-year-olds interested."

"Yuck!" she said.

She knew she was projecting her own frustration, her own misery: only last month, her live-in partner, Patrick, had been fired, after being accused of "inappropriate behaviour" by three female co-workers. He had denied it all, but Denise had taken the accusation as condemnation. Not only of him, but of herself. Her scrapbook was full of men she had chosen, who were the life of the party, who were great in bed, and who in the end had disappointed her simply by being themselves. She had silently packed her things into boxes and moved in with her mother. And quickly, her father's actions had become magnified.

From Bangkok, Denise found the Chiang Mai hotel online, phoned the number, and gave her father's name. No, the clerk said, he wasn't there at present, but he remembered him well. "A friendly fellow," the man said. "He stayed here maybe a month." And yes, he was with a woman who lived in a village south of Bangkok. The clerk thought they might have gone there. No, he couldn't exactly remember the name of it, but it was near Phetchaburi. On a beach.

And now, here they are, no closer to finding her father, and almost ready to give up and abandon him to whatever life he has now invented for himself. When they're within a block of their hotel, Denise's phone vibrates in her pocket. She pulls it out. Patrick. She's been ignoring his calls, not answering his email.

Guy gives her a questioning look.

"You go ahead, okay?" she says. "I'll catch up." She waits until he's out of earshot.

"I miss you," Patrick says, when he hears her voice.

"I'm in Thailand," she says. "Looking for Dad." Then she adds, "How are you doing?"

He pauses. "Not so well," he says. "There've been more... allegations. It's a frenzy...."

Her stomach tightens, but she says nothing.

"Of course, they're false," he says. "I don't know what's going to happen. I feel as if my life is going down the drain."

Again, she doesn't answer.

"Don't be mad," he says. "I want you to come home."

Home, she thinks. How quickly that concept changes. She sighs. "I don't know."

"I need you in my corner," he says.

"I've got to go," she says, thinking he didn't say he hired an attorney; he didn't say he's going to defend himself in court.

"Denise?"

She hangs up and puts the phone back in her pocket.

They're lying in a king-sized bed in a bungalow facing the beach, staring at the teak ceiling, the lazy turning of the fan. It's early morning and the air echoes with the cooing of spotted doves, the *ko-el, ko-el* of a mating bird, the screech of starlings and the barbets' hammerings. The incoming waves are louder this morning, as if a storm were brewing. Guy reaches for the water bottle beside Denise, his arm across her breasts. Denise shuts her eyes, thinking of Patrick in their apartment back home. His pale thin arms. The surprise, the hurt in his eyes while she packed. Two years, she thinks. How is it so easy to let it all go? Perhaps, she thinks, there was something there I intuited. Perhaps I knew something was not right. But what? Am I only making excuses? Is this a way out?

"Hey," Guy says, stroking her cheek.

She opens her eyes. "Hey yourself."

He turns towards her, leans on his elbow. "So, what are we going to do?" he says, as if this is a conversation they've been having.

Denise runs her fingers along the soft underside of his arm. She wishes she could fall in love with him, that he were the type of man she could depend on, the type of man who would not disappoint her. Instead she says, "We're going to find my dad."

"That's not what I meant, and you know it."

She closes her eyes again. "I want to find my dad and take him home."

He falls onto his back. "Fine," he says.

Later, in early evening, they wander into the village, following the discord of familiar songs to a bar facing the ocean, with a karaoke setup against an inner wall whose shelves are heaped with liquor bottles. Half the bar's tables are arranged on a wooden patio, with festive yellow and orange umbrellas beside them. Candles quiver on tabletops, and floodlights define the perimeter.

Denise and Guy settle into wobbly white plastic chairs, and idly leaf through laminated spiral notebooks of song titles — mostly standard oldies and American and British pop tunes from the '70s and '80s. Through the speakers, a man's voice warbles through a desiccated version of "My Way." Denise watches the singing man nervously, aware of the My Way Killings, which have taken place throughout Asia. Here in Thailand, not so long ago, someone shot twelve harmonizing singers, apparently offended by their enthusiastic dissonance. She wonders what it is about the song that raises blood pressures and encourages rage. Surely not only off-key singing. Could it be the song's lyrics, with their defiant attitude? I did it my way!

Her phone vibrates. Patrick again.

Guy raises his eyebrows at her.

She sets the phone on the table, where it continues to vibrate.

"Are you going to give him a chance to explain?" Guy says.

"There's nothing left to explain," Denise says.

Guy looks at her. "What about due process?"

Of course, she's considered this. Not only concerning Patrick, but concerning anyone who has been accused of something. Yet she can't bring herself to say that she can continue living with Patrick given the nature of the accusations. Not that she knows specifically what he's done. What exactly constitutes "inappropriate behaviour"? She thinks of possibilities: sexual innuendoes? Dirty jokes? Commenting on women's clothing? Or could it be bullying? "Behaviour" implies attitude, and attitude is subjective. She shakes her head. Whatever he's done, someone has decided it is serious enough to fire him. "I'm sure I'll see due process if Patrick pursues it."

"I hope you know what you're doing," Guy says.

She shrugs and sips her beer. What she does know is that, if Patrick does defend himself or sue for defamation, even if he wins, their relationship is over. How could he want to be with a partner who has not supported and trusted him? Yes, she knows what she's doing. She's made her choice.

Slowly, people file into the bar, mostly young Thais in jeans and hoodies. The waiter scoops the two spiral notebooks from Denise and Guy's table and drops them onto two other tables.

Denise and Guy have heard that a number of *farangs* congregate here most days, and they're hoping that one of them will know her father. However, now that they are here, Denise can't imagine men like her father sitting through grating karaoke versions of popular songs.

"I'll go ask the bartender about the men," Guy says, and when he returns, he says, "They do come here, but earlier in the day. They're pretty well gone the minute karaoke starts up."

Then, as if they've willed a miracle, four middle-aged Caucasian men and three Thai girls approach. They choose a spot as far as possible from the karaoke machine, push two tables together and settle around them. One of the men waves for the waiter, beckoning with two fingers, something Denise knows is offensive in Thai culture.

"I'm going to go talk to them," Denise says, and Guy shrugs.

She gets up and approaches. Close up now, she can see that three of the men are on the far side of sixty, maybe more, and the three Thai girls have fresh, unlined faces. One wears a Hello Kitty! T-shirt and clutches a white stuffed Hello Kitty! with a red bow in its hair. The stuffed cat has no mouth. The fourth man is younger, maybe in his fifties, definitely the alpha here. Denise forces herself to speak to them.

"Excuse me," she says. "Do you live here?"

The younger man sits between two of the girls. He smiles, leans back in his seat, thighs spread, and nods. "What's your name?" he asks, in an American drawl. He looks like a young Arnold Schwarzenegger, blond hair tinged white at the temples and large, straight white teeth. His arms are spread out on the back of the seats beside him, as if he were about to hug both girls who are with his friends. "Would you like to join us for a drink?"

"I'm looking for someone," she says. "Maybe you can help me."

"Sure. Come and join us."

She keeps her lips slightly upturned into the semblance of a smile. "I'm with someone," she says, motioning to Guy. She reaches into her purse for a photograph of her father. "Do you know this man?" she asks.

The man takes the photo and stares at it for a moment. He passes the photo around to the other three men, who all look at each other, as if trying to make a decision.

"Do you know him?" Denise repeats.

"We might," the first man says, returning the photo. "Is there a problem?" The men are now sitting up straighter, staring intently at her in a brotherhood of suspicion.

"I'm not here to make trouble," she says. "I just need to talk to him. He's my dad."

The men eye each other once more, making a silent decision. "We could pass along the information," one suggests.

"Could you see if he'll agree to meet me? It's really important."

The man shrugs. "I'll see what I can do. Try coming back tomorrow. But earlier. Around 4:00."

"Fine, fine. That would be good. Thank you so much for your help."

"Don't thank me yet."

Denise lets her breath come out all at once. After all this, she's found him. She walks out past the table area, onto the beach, aware suddenly of the warm air, the surging tide's rhythmic gasps, the chirping crickets, the croaking of frogs. In front of her, the beach is deserted. A cruise ship skims the horizon, and here and there, past the breakwater's beacons, lights of fishing boats flicker on waves. She takes out her cellphone.

"Now would you join us for that drink?" a voice says behind her.

She whirls, startled, plunging the cellphone into the depths of her pocket. "No thank you," she says.

The man stares at her for a moment, shifting his weight from foot to foot. He looks more like a tourist than a resident in his expensive grey linen pants and white shirt. "Are you going to make trouble for your dad?"

Her body stiffens. "I just want to talk to him."

"Your dad is happy here," the man says. "It's a wonderful place." He smiles, all teeth showing.

"Look," she says. "Right now, I'm trying to make a phone call." She raises her eyebrows at him.

"Okay. Sorry. I was just trying to be friendly."

She turns back seaward, and rolls her eyes. She hears rather than sees the man retreat, his feet crunching the sand. She pulls out her phone again. What if she's wrong? What if Patrick is telling the truth? Should she be giving him a chance to tell his side of the story? No, she tells herself firmly. I will not be like those women who remain willfully blind to their partners' transgressions in spite of mounting evidence against them. But do accusations necessarily mean guilt? She stuffs the phone back in her pocket and returns to Guy.

The three Thai girls are gone, the men leftovers, regulars. They joke with the waiter and shout out to the bartender. They are, Denise thinks, probably retired embassy or company men, who have middle-aged, exhausted ex-wives back in Britain or Australia, or the US or other Western countries, and now are married to Thai teenagers who bear them babies and can barely speak their language. In Chiang Mai alone, she has read, there are 40,000 resident expats, often paired with young women forty to fifty years younger than themselves. She wonders if the girls have lovers they meet while the men congregate in bars. She remembers herself at eighteen, constantly in and out of passionate love with young men her own age.

The following afternoon, the expats are scattered around the bar in groups of four to six, playing backgammon or cards, beer sweating in glasses in front of them. They all look up when Denise and Guy come in, and a couple raise their hands in greeting.

"I'm going to check out the game," Guy says, when they're settled at a table from which they can see the entrance.

Denise watches him go and stand over a backgammon table. She is the only woman in the bar, the pack of men staking territory, or protecting it. She thinks of the rejected wives, sisters, brothers, children, grandchildren, of her own mother, despondent, at home. She wonders if the men abandoned them or were pushed out. The men eye the door, glance at her. Do they think she poses a threat? Have others, like her, come to disrupt their new lives?

It takes her a moment to recognize her father in his long baggy cargo shorts and T-shirt, her father who spent his life in suits and ties, working for an oil company. He stops at the edge of the bar and peers in until he sees her, then resolutely moves towards her. Denise stands up, and Guy joins her immediately. Hidden behind her father is a young Thai girl. Though she prepared for it, Denise feels her stomach clench.

Her father embraces her quickly. She introduces him to Guy, and the men shake hands. Then her father moves aside. "Denise," he says. "I'd like you to meet Kwang." He pushes a pregnant girl forward.

The girl folds her hands, as if in prayer, and bows slightly.

Denise makes herself smile. "Hello." She does a quick calculation in her head. When this child is ten, her father will be seventy-seven. Has he thought of that? She shudders.

Her father pulls out a chair for Kwang, then sits down as well. "What brings you here?" he asks, challenging her. The men in the room are silent, and her father's voice is soft against the backdrop of piped-in music and the waves' rhythmic swells.

"Dad," Denise says. "We need to talk." She pauses. "Privately." She motions toward the beach with her head.

The girl stares from Denise to her father. "She is daughter?" she asks.

"Yes," her father says, "my daughter." He looks sheepish.

None of them say anything for a moment. Then the girl slowly stands up, clutching her abdomen. "I go. You talk." She turns to Denise and Guy. "Nice meeting you." Again she folds her hands, bows, then goes to stand at the edge of the bar, where one of the men pulls back a chair for her at an empty table. Denise can feel multiple eyes on her.

"That went well," Guy says, raising an eyebrow.

"Why are you here?" her father says, his voice fierce.

"Mom —" Denise begins.

"What's between your mother and me," her father says, "has nothing to do with you."

"You can't be serious! It has everything to do with me. I'm part of your family!" She says it loudly enough for the men in the room to perk up.

"I know you don't understand," her father says. "But I've started a new life here."

Guy puts a hand on her arm, his fingers both soothing and irritating.

"Are you ever going to come home?" she says.

He looks towards Kwang and smiles at her.

Denise's mouth feels as if it's full of cotton. She has been practising all the things she'll say to him to remind him of their life together, and now, it all seems pointless. "How old is she, Dad?" she says.

Her father narrows his eyes. "Age doesn't matter. Happiness matters."

Denise glares at him incredulously. "Whose happiness are we talking about here?" she says. "Your wife's? Your children's? Or maybe that young girl who could be your granddaughter?"

"Denise—" Guy begins.

"Oh, I get it. It's your happiness that's important," Denise finishes.

Her father stands up. "This is not getting us anywhere," he says and draws out a business card from his shirt pocket. "If you really want to talk, you know where to find me." He throws the card on the table and leaves.

Denise watches him go, imagining herself clicking the minus sign on a screen, making the focus recede into the background until it's unrecognizable. That's what we've become to him, she thinks. Invisible.

She and Guy finish their beer in silence. There's nothing to add, nothing to take away. The expats continue their card or backgammon games, heads bent over their hands, no longer worried or threatened. Denise picks up her father's card and slips it in her purse. She feels a depth of sadness for him suddenly, and swallows back the lump rising in her throat. Perhaps, she thinks, we're all willing to trade something for what we yearn.

Outside, the air feels cooler, calmer, especially the further they get from the bar. She and Guy walk for ten minutes or so, until finally they hear only the drone of crickets and grasshoppers and frogs in the marshland. As they round a corner, they come to an empty field stippled with dogs. These are a younger pack, alert, less scraggly. As they approach, the dogs slowly stand and come forward, until they are lined up like guards skirting the road. Denise instinctively moves closer to the opposite side of the road and avoids looking at the dogs.

One of the dogs separates from the rest and boldly takes a couple of steps forward. He's sturdy, with a short-hair coat in various hues of brown and black. His face is thin and pointed, his black ears erect.

Denise touches Guy's sleeve. "Move slowly. Don't look at him."

"You go ahead," Guy says. "Get past them."

The lead dog advances another step and snarls. Denise jumps, and both she and Guy quicken their pace. Tail up in the air, the dog takes another cautious step closer, this time growling deeply, teeth bared. Following its lead, the other dogs begin to bark furiously.

Denise and Guy stand tall, yelling and waving their arms, trying to look bigger and less frightened than they feel, but the dogs continue to edge forward, forcing them back.

"What are we going to do?" Denise cries above the cacophony of dogs barking.

Dusk turns the sky gunmetal grey. A generator hums into motion, and in the distance the rumble of a motorcycle fades into a Buddhist incantation, a chanting of monks, while a skein of whistling ducks flies overhead.

*It doesn't matter who my father was.*
*It matters who I remember he was.*

—Anne Sexton

# GHOST MEN

It begins with a haunting, her father appearing in her dreams night after night. He's his younger self — one Skye only recognizes from black-and-white photos — a handsome, smiling man of thirty-nine, the same age she is now, newly married, her mother at his side. He's trying to tell her something, and she leans towards him, focusing on his face and concentrating on the sound of his words, which echo and swirl into unintelligible turbulence. Night after night he emerges in different guises: a black minister's robe, a strange military uniform with indecipherable insignia on his cap and sleeves, a tuxedo, as if he were ready for a party. Sometimes he whispers to her while he himself is sleeping, as if within his dreams he's reaching out to her inside her dreams, as if by meeting in a different dimension, they'll communicate.

Tonight, his shouts yank her out of her sleep. She sits up, disoriented. His voice continues outside her window, hysterical, shrill, close. What's he saying? Fully awake now, she springs up and, without turning on any lights, runs to the apartment door, to double-check the locks, then the windows and sliding-glass patio door. The voice grows louder, and she picks up her cell. Should she call 911? Would they think her overly dramatic? After all, nothing has happened. Not yet. The shouting increases in volume. She fingers 911, but doesn't press the green telephone icon to set the call in motion. Huddled at the edge of the window, she tries to spy who's out there. The voice terrifies her; its proximity terrifies her. Why is she living on the bottom floor of a three-storey apartment building? She's been warned not to do that. She's heard stories of serial rapists who stalk women in ground-floor apartments. Like the recent one of the Golden State Killer Joseph James DeAngelo — *dark angel* — who raped fifty women, murdered twelve others, and burglarized over 100 homes; who evaded capture for over forty years. What kind of man is capable of that? she thinks, huddling at the side of the sliding door, cell in hand.

Beyond the postage-stamp patio, a four-foot yew hedge separates her from the sidewalk, on the other side of which gnarled arbutus shelter the sidewalk from the road. Shelter intruders too. Anxiety tightens her chest.

The man comes into view, and she instinctively steps back. He's tall, dishevelled, eyes glazed in fury, dragging a dirty blue windbreaker behind him, gesticulating with one hand, as if he were menacing someone, his voice loud and incomprehensible.

She looks at her cell. Who can she call? Not her parents, from whom she's estranged, not any of her Facebook friends, not even her best friend Paris, who lives across town, and who would surely tell her that she's being silly and paranoid.

The man is alone, intent on his private demons. He marches past her window; his voice billows, then slowly recedes with his steps.

Shaken, she lets out her breath all at once, unaware that she's been holding it.

Back in bed, she falls into a troubled sleep, and this time is awakened by the sound of Paris's car honking outside. She should be grateful for the ride, for not having to take a bus and Skytrain to work. Instead, she's late again. She sends Paris an apologetic text, then quickly washes and dresses. Fifteen minutes later, she's making up excuses to give her boss, knowing full well that he'll expect her to make up the time.

"Why do you sabotage yourself? Just quit the damn job," Paris says later that evening. She's a take-control person Skye can trust to do all the right things, whatever they are. Paris is Skye's antithesis: while Skye types numbers into Excel, Paris blasts into the past like a bloodhound, tracking lost fathers and mothers, ancestors, lineage; she trades in boyfriends at will, owns her own business.

"That's easy for you to say," Skye says. It's the first Thursday of the month, when a group of them come together for gourmet dinners in each other's homes on a rotating basis. They began with ad hoc meetings after Paris's father died, as a way to support Paris, then as they got to know each other better, turned the meetings into dinners, and now they've morphed into a kind of gourmet club, though they don't all show up for every meal. Tonight, six of them — Skye, Paris, Zoë, Ellen, Ferris and Richard — are seated around Paris's dining room table. Clara is in Italy, Denise in Thailand, and Vivian has gone to Toronto to visit her mother. "You're not the one living paycheque to paycheque." Skye stares at the framed platinum and gold records lining the walls, the shrine to Paris's dead father. "I can't even afford an apartment on another floor," she says, and goes on to tell them about the night-time rager.

"Why don't you move to another place, then?" Paris says, her voice like a pin pricking Skye in all the wrong places.

Skye doesn't bother to answer. She sighs loudly and imagines herself packing her few things into boxes, quitting her job, and living on the street, begging for quarters, an escapee from a life of commitments and reproaches.

"Sometimes," Richard says, "moving to another place doesn't solve anything. You simply take your problems with you." He brushes imaginary lint from the sleeve of his polo shirt, which earlier he told them is "a Sunspel Riviera originally created for Daniel Craig for his role as James Bond in *Casino Royale*," though none of them could recall that film.

"Sometimes," Ellen says, "not moving doesn't solve anything either." She pours herself a glass of white wine and leans back in her chair. "I've decided to go back to work part-time," she says, and everyone beams.

Skye nods. Before his failed suicide attempt, Richard roved from one of his houses to the next, and Ellen spent years as a shut-in. Neither of their problems disappeared, but their responses to them have changed. What Skye really wants is to shed her entire life as if it were an ugly outfit she bought and now wants to discard.

"I broke up with Lawrence," Zoë says suddenly, and they all turn to her. She has been yada-yada-ing about her long-distance lover as long as they've known her. "After all these years, the minute I gave him an ultimatum, he divorced his wife." She picks up her wineglass as if to make a toast, and they all pick up theirs. "But not for me," she says. "He's got a new woman." She lifts the glass and drinks. The rest lower theirs.

"Whaaaat?" Paris frowns.

"What a jerk!" Skye says, shaking her head. "Wouldn't it be great if we could shed people at will?" she says, thinking *Sylvain, Brent, Father.*

"Yeah well…" Zoë sighs.

Ellen pats her arm. "Never mind. He's not worth it."

"I just keep thinking about all the wasted years," Zoë says. "I should have listened to you all." She pauses. "Do you think I should call him?"

"NO!" they all say almost in unison.

"My parents are having their fortieth anniversary," Skye says, "and my brother wants me to go see them." She tells them that two weeks before, she stopped answering her landline, as if her silence could annihilate the voices. Like Orwell's *1984* in which Newspeak restricts language, removes words to limit thought. Abolish the word *snow* and snow will vanish. Eliminate *love, fear, anxiety*. She's exercising Newhear by removing voices. Out of sound, out of mind. Her voicemail is full now, which means there will be no more additions, no more demands she cannot satisfy, though the haunting continues.

"How come we didn't know you had a brother?" Paris says, frowning. "Is he older? Younger?"

"Much younger," she says. "I barely know him." Her brother found her through Facebook several years ago, and they connected sporadically through messaging and texts. Joe is a friendly stranger — having been three or four when she left home — whose knowledge of her is limited to what her parents have told him. She assumes they demonized her, but she doesn't question him, not wanting to expose herself. She and Joe have Skyped, but have not met face-to-face, due in part to distance — Joe's family lives in Las Vegas, close to Mesquite, where her parents relocated after her father retired — and in part due to her unwillingness to dredge up the past.

"I thought you were Canadian," Ferris says. He's sitting next to Paris, and now casually drapes his arm on the back of her chair. "How come your parents live in the US?"

"My father's American," Skye says. "My mother is Canadian, and I was born in Vancouver. We've lived on both sides of the border at different times." She stares at Paris, questioning.

Paris leans forward, and Ferris retrieves his arm.

"How do you feel about it?" Zoë says, and they all focus on Skye.

"I don't know." Skye shakes her head.

"Well, I think you should go," Paris says. "You've no idea how lucky you are to have living parents."

"Am I?" Skye says, thinking how wistful Paris's voice sounds, how much she yearns for parents, unlike Skye, who hasn't wanted to see hers for twenty-three years.

"I'll go with you if you like," Paris says. "I could use a break. We could take a week, drive down the coast, play a few slot machines in Vegas, lounge in a spa…whatever, and end up in Mesquite."

Back in her own apartment later that night, Skye listens to the phone messages once more.

"Skye, please," her brother Joe's voice says. "Is it too much to ask you to think of Mom and Dad for once? Put them ahead of you."

He says, *You need to come, even if it's just for one night. You can stay in a hotel.*

He says, *Hasn't this gone on long enough? It's a chance to reconcile.*

He says, *Whatever happened years ago, you need to let it go.*

He says, *It's their 40th anniversary, for god's sake!*

He says, *They're getting old. Mom is heartbroken.*

He says, *I'll never forgive you if they die without this family reconciling.*

He says, *Please, Christina. Do this for them. Do this for Mom.*

Skye's stomach clenches around the words *Dad* and *Mom*. Why aren't they dead? she thinks. She plays and replays the messages, unnerved, *Mom* and *Dad* ricocheting in her head, as she regresses to her teenage years, rebelling against her father, against his fundamentalist religious views, his night-time hauntings, his stifling control of both her and her mother. He locked her out of the house, finally, when at sixteen she was arrested for chaining herself in front of a logging truck to protest the cutting of an old growth forest. Her mother came to bail her out, but her father did not allow her back into the house. Skye went to stay with a friend, and within a few weeks, met Sylvain — a charismatic forty-something man with Charles Manson eyes.

She checks for emails, but finds none. She logs into Second Life, but suddenly the familiar hand logo looks like a STOP sign. She turns off the computer and speed-dials her therapist instead, then hangs up before the first ring. It's the middle of the night, for god's sakes. Get a grip! she tells herself and stares out at the multitude of empty offices in the buildings around her, their lights ablaze, wondering how many migrating birds will mistake the artificial lights for stars. It's hard at times to distinguish artifice from candour, love from lust, baubles from substance. She seems eternally attracted to the artificial aura of men, as if she were heeding mistaken signals, like ants following a pheromone trail of pesticide to their deaths.

What clinches her decision to go, despite her apprehension, is a photo Joe emails of his three-year-old daughter in their father's arms.

"I'm glad we're doing this," Paris says, as Vancouver recedes in the rear-view mirror. "I haven't been on a road trip in years."

"Me neither," Skye says, thinking she's never been on a road trip, not in the sense that Paris means.

"Aunt Fiona really liked camping, so when I was a child, the two of us would head out every weekend and holiday. Pitch a tent, cook over a Coleman stove, hike around. It was a great way to see the country."

Skye imagines Paris and her aunt on the road, following Paris's father gig to gig, though she knows this is not what happened. "What about your dad?" she asks.

"What about him?" Paris says, then she glances at Skye. "Did your family do road trips too?"

"Not those kind," Skye says. "My father was a minister. He preached on Sundays and holidays. Our weekend picnics were dry sandwiches and coffee in the church basement. That's not a great way to see the country."

They are both silent after that, each in her own thoughts, as they inch toward the border crossing. Skye stares out the open window at the dividing line between Canada and the US. How easy it is to define borders on the physical landscape — draw a line, erect a fence or a wall, guard it from both sides. No such definition in one's own borders, the flimsy defence, the barricades scaled from the inside. She has spent a lot of her adult life in toxic relationships, beginning with a commune that advocated sexual freedom, which meant the leader had his choice of girls and rewarded the boys with one of them when they particularly pleased him. Skye, being the youngest, was a favourite reward. After seven years, she finally left the commune with Brent, one of the men, imagining the two of them as a couple living a cliché life in a bungalow surrounded by a white picket fence. However, it didn't take long for Brent, who had no job or work prospects, to suggest she turn a few tricks. "What's the difference?" he said. "It isn't as if you haven't had multiple partners." She spent the next two years with him. She can hardly bear to think of any of it now without spiralling into a panic attack.

It took night school, college, and a lot of counselling before she could even imagine herself trusting another man. The perfect solution arose in 2008, when she discovered and joined Second Life, the alternative world making front-page news with virtual stores and virtual embassies, virtual money and virtual people who could not harm her. There, in this perfect parallel universe, she was Eva. At one point, Skye was featured in a newspaper Focus as the woman whose Second Life had become larger than her real life, so much so that she no longer left the house except to work. "I can't wait to get home so I can return to my normal life," the quote read, right under the photograph of her cartoon avatar, walking a two-dimensional dog along a two-dimensional street, her blank avatar eyes staring straight ahead and unsmiling. Fortunately, when she met Zoë and Paris in 2012, they staged an intervention, although Skye still secretly logs on to what nowadays is a ghost town.

They continue past the border for a little over an hour, and as they approach Burlington, Skye suddenly sits up. "Let's do the Cascades Loop."

"I thought we were going down the coast," Paris says, but she slows down.

"I know. I know. But this will be worth it, I promise." She points. "It's the next exit."

Paris raises her eyebrows, then shrugs and veers onto the exit which takes them onto Highway 20. "Any particular reason?" she asks.

"Just want to see if a place still exists," Skye says. They are now heading inland, past Sedro Wooley on a deserted highway parallel to the Skagit River. She had been on this highway many years before, huddled in a van under blankets, her heart open and trusting. Naïve. She draws in her breath. She's never revealed this part of her life. Not even to Paris. A whorl of anxiety flutters in her chest.

"A place or a person?"

"Both." Skye took a deep breath. "It's just a place I spent some time at, years ago."

"What, like a summer camp?"

"Not exactly," Skye says, then stares out the window.

"How far along is it?"

"Sixty, seventy, eighty miles. I don't know. I'll know it when I see it, warn you when we're close." Paris's eyes bore into her profile.

"Is it a man we're looking for?" Paris asks.

"We're not looking for anyone, though yes, there is a man."

"Were you in a relationship with this man?"

Skye hesitates. "Sort of," she says. "But so long ago, I hardly remember him that way."

"I know what you mean," Paris says. "Sometimes, exes turn into friends or enemies, and it's hard to remember them in any other way." She pauses. "I've got one like that. Paul. I can only think of him as an old friend, though we did once have a romantic relationship."

While Paris talks about Paul, the six-month fling they had in their twenties, Skye thinks about the upcoming reunion, trying to rid herself of the familiar foreboding. Surely her father was also kind in those first sixteen years. She fights against glimpses of herself in her father's arms, of picnics by the sea, of barbeques in the backyard of their house, of her father steadying her on her first bicycle; fights these memories, preferring to recall his sternness, his pronouncements, the night-time hauntings, her injuries. Memory, she thinks, is elusive, not firm, but altered by time, like the earth's surface, softened or hardened, charred or greened, depending on the person's bias, or culture, or any of a hundred other circumstances.

About three hours into their journey, as the Skagit River widens to Gorge Lake, Skye peers out the window. "Slow down a bit," Skye says. "I think we're coming up to it." Her heart begins to pound. Soon, she points to what looks like an abandoned gravel road to the left of the highway.

Paris brakes and turns onto it. Tire tracks are exposed, but clumps of grass and weeds grow between them. They proceed slowly, until several miles in, the road comes to an abrupt end in front of a rotting wooden gate. "Now what?" Paris asks.

Skye has the door half-open already. "Come on. I'll explain as we go. Follow me."

"How do you know this place even exists?"

Skye shakes her head. She unlatches the wooden gate and pushes it open. A surge of emotions threaten to overcome her, and she hears her father's voice in her head, Sylvain's voice, men's voices, all calling out. She wants to go to them, to flee. She presses her fingers into her temples.

"What's the matter?" Paris asks, her arm circling Skye's shoulders.

"It's…" Skye takes a deep breath, and silently repeats the mantra: *You cannot control me, you cannot control me*, using one of the therapist-suggested coping mechanisms. *This is not real, this is not real.*

"Are you all right? What can I do?" Paris says.

The voices abruptly stop, and Skye looks up. She strains towards the voices, but hears only the swishing of leaves in the trees. More and more, these voices haunt her like a mirage, the past projected into her brain, distorted and displaced. She finds a fallen log and sits down heavily. "I'm okay now," she says, pressing her hand to her chest. In counselling, she began to understand that she's in some sort of arrested development. Arrested. Like a criminal. Searching, perhaps, for a father to defy. She thinks about PTSD and wars and authoritarian regimes, and fathers and men.

Paris continues to stare at her, alarmed.

"Really, I'm fine," Skye says, smiling to reassure her. "It's this place. Bad vibes. It got to me."

"What's going on?" Paris says. "Where are we going?"

"Trust me, okay?" Skye gets up, and leads the way down the path, then into the woods, where a less-visible trail leads away from the gate.

"When you met my dad," Paris says, when they've been walking for a bit, "in the support group, I mean, what was he like?"

Skye stops and turns to her. "We didn't know him like you knew him…." She thinks of her own father, the Minister, of how he must appear to others, of how difficult it is to know what's really going on inside a home.

"I hardly knew him," Paris says. "Sporadic visits...until he got sick, and even then..." Her voice trails off.

"When we met him, he was a rock star, you know? We were all a little in awe. But he was nice — "

"Was he drinking? Detoxed?"

Skye shakes her head. "I don't know. He seemed normal to me, just unhappy." She turns and begins up the trail again.

"Did he ever mention me?" Paris asks.

Skye stops again. She doesn't recall Cole ever mentioning a daughter, but she had her own problems at the time, and anyway, it was so long ago. "I'm sure he must have," she says, "but I was pretty screwed up, so I've blanked all that stuff out." She pauses. "Sorry. I wish I could give you more."

"It's okay," Paris says. "I just wondered, that's all."

They resume walking and a half hour later, various crude wooden buildings emerge, half-hidden within tall grasses, brush and pines, as if reclaimed by the forest. Most of the roofs are sagging, obscured by moss; porch planks have rotted away leaving gaping jagged rectangles; crude stone chimneys have been reduced to rubble; a door hangs on one hinge. A ghost town.

"What is this place?" Paris says, tramping through the underbrush to peer through dirty cracked windows. "Is this your childhood home? Did you grow up here?"

For seven years, she lived in this commune situated at the end of a gravel road, miles from the nearest town. She was the youngest of Sylvain's "children," among the twenty young women and nine young men who worshipped and feared him. When she first arrived, he had had a "baptism" in which he cast away her past, and renamed her Skye. Sometimes at night, one of the men shouted in the forest — a plaintive call, broken, supplicating, then slowly surging with rage. She imagined Sylvain, whip in hand, subjugating the young man. When she tiptoed to the window, however, she saw only one figure silhouetted against the sky, fists raised against an unseen foe. A bad trip, she told herself, having witnessed many. Magic mushrooms, windowpane LSD, all types of pharmaceuticals to laden the brain, to escape oneself. How has she escaped unscathed, she wonders now. Or perhaps not totally unscathed, given the constant low-grade anxiety, which sometimes verges on paranoia. The hauntings, the voices, her father, the man the other morning, for example, was he real? Did he really stalk past her window?

"It's a commune," Skye says, and explains a little of this to Paris now. "I lived here from sixteen to twenty-three."

Paris lets out a soft whistle. "You're kidding. I've heard of such things, but didn't know anyone — "

"No, that's the point. They don't want anyone to know." She walks from building to building, pointing out, explaining. "This was the women's dorm," she says. The remains of three mouldy mattresses slouch against a wall. "This was the kitchen and dining area." She points to the rusted stove, the mouse droppings on the counters. "And that half-building over there was a stable where two horses were kept. The shack beside it is where the men slept." She pauses. "It looks so desperate now, but it didn't feel desperate in those days."

Paris follows her quietly. Now and then, she pats Skye's back. "Why didn't you tell us?" she says finally.

Skye shrugs. "What difference would it have made?"

"We might have helped, you know?" Paris says. "It's about sharing."

"We all have our own problems," Skye says. "And only we can deal with them." She turns to stare at the detritus around her. "And these," she says, pointing to the largest building, "were Sylvain's quarters. He was the only one with a private space. This is where…" They approach the decaying porch, the padlocked door. The windows are black with dirt and dust, impossible to see through. She wonders when the commune was abandoned and how.

"How old was this guy?" Paris asks.

"In his forties."

"And you were teenagers? A pedophile, really," Paris says. "It's a wonder he never got put away."

"We all adored him," Skye says. "I don't know why, but I know back then, we would have protected him with our lives."

"You were brainwashed!" Paris says.

Skye shrugs. Brainwashed. With love. By love. Sylvain found her at a bus stop and offered her a place to stay, helped her into a van where two teenage girls fawned over her. She settled into his flophouse on the outskirts of the city, at first sharing a mattress with another girl, then moving into Sylvain's bedroom where he love bombed her with attention so that she felt *seen* and understood. He convinced her that now she was in a true family that would never abandon her. Once committed, she was taken to the commune in the country, and she was rewarded for good behaviour and subtly punished for "wayward" questioning. She learned to feel guilty if she deviated in any way from what Sylvain wanted. And she bent herself to his wishes.

Paris sighs. "Textbook techniques," she murmurs. "You were little more than a child."

"A child in a woman's body." Skye says. "I was…I don't know." She takes a deep breath. "I wanted to please him…I loved him!" Blood rushes to her cheeks.

Paris gives her a sympathetic look.

They are both silent for a moment, then Paris pats her arm. "I'm sorry."

Skye shakes her head. "It's okay," she says. "Long gone," though her heart is pounding.

Paris watches her for a moment, as if to decipher if she really is okay. Then she grasps Skye's arm. "Let's get out of here," she says. "This place gives me the creeps." She begins to retrace her steps to the trail.

"No, wait," Skye says. "There's one more place."

"You don't really think he'd still be here?"

"Why not? This was his kingdom," Skye says. "Unless he's dead or got sent to jail, I think he'd stay here. He is that kind of crazy."

Paris shrugs and follows Skye further into the woods, where they pursue a trail, the entrance of which is hidden by tall brush and grasses. This path, however, is well worn.

Skye sees him first, in the clearing, surrounded by Douglas firs. He is bent over a stump, chopping firewood, his arms toned and muscular. From the back, he looks young and fit, as if he's made a deal with the devil, and somewhere in one of the abandoned buildings, his portrait withers against a wall. *Father*! her inner voice calls out, but she stops herself in time. "Sylvain," she says as calmly as she can.

He turns abruptly and gives them a wary look. For a moment, she thinks he might run. His face is tanned and his black hair tied in a ponytail which reaches halfway down his back. He is the Sylvain of the past, the one she loved.

"I'm looking for Sylvain," Skye says.

He frowns, the axe still held in both hands. He has the same blue piercing eyes. "Are you one of his hippie followers from ages ago?"

She hears the dismissal in his voice. "Is he alive?" she asks, thinking Sylvain must now be in his seventies.

He stares at her, as if sizing her up. "I suppose you want some kind of closure," he says finally, setting the axe down.

"Punishment or revenge is more like it."

"Stand in line," he says.

"Where is the bastard?" Paris asks.

The man shrugs. "My dad got old. He's not here any more. He moved on. Maybe you should too."

He seems unperturbed. Doesn't he realize the impact his father had on so many young lives? This man is in his mid to late thirties. He must be the product of an earlier marriage, or union. No one gave birth during her tenure at the commune.

"Do you have an address?" Skye asks, though she knows it's futile.

"Daddy, Daddy!" a voice calls out. "There's someone coming!" A girl emerges from the woods. She's no more than ten, wearing cut-off blue jeans and a halter top that exposes her midriff. Her long dark hair swings in a braid down her back. "Oh," she says when she sees them. She hurries to the man and presses herself into his side, stands partly behind him, as if afraid.

"And who are you?" Skye asks, a déjà vu moment clouding her brain. The young girl, the love. Her therapist explained that these moments can stem from just one fragment of a familiar experience, tricking her into thinking she's reliving an entire event that has already occurred.

"This is my daughter," the man says, in a tone that sounds defensive to Skye. He puts his arm around the girl, who buries her face into his stomach.

"One of your children?" Skye says, her voice tight and high-pitched. She stares hard at the two of them, trying to make sense of this.

"Is there a wife?" Paris says. "What's going on here?"

The man abruptly releases the girl. "Go back to the house," he says. "I'll take care of this."

The girl looks at them for a moment, then turns to leave. The man gives her a little push towards the path. "Go on," he says, then when she's gone, he pulls his axe out of the stump, and waves it in the air. "And now, if you don't mind, get off my property."

Skye steps back. "I hope for your sake there's a wife here," she says.

He starts towards her. Paris takes her arm and pulls her away. The man watches them impassively. They turn and retrace their steps along the pathway, looking back only when they reach the mildewed gate. No one follows. Skye kicks one of the rotted slats, and it breaks off and falls with a thud. She steps over it, then she and Paris walk the rest of the way to the car. As soon as they have cell reception, Paris calls 911 and gives the police coordinates and information.

"If that is what I think it is, he'll get what's coming to him," she says.

"She's too young. Maybe he really is her dad, and they're living a back-to-the-land utopian existence."

"Maybe," Paris says. "But shouldn't there be a mom?"

Skye shakes her head. For the past three years, she's been volunteering at a battered women's shelter. The ugly stories are familiar and seemingly without end. Women and girls are being exploited in every which way, no matter how much the media speaks of a culture change. She sighs. "That was deeply unsatisfying."

"What did you expect?" Paris asks.

"More than that," Skye says, though she doesn't really know what. She stares out the window at the thick forest beside her. Beyond the "Highway Closed in Winter" sign lies Diablo, a small company town surrounding the Diablo Dam, one of three along the Skagit River. She wonders if Sylvain chose to live near Diablo, or whether it was a curious coincidence. They continue along the highway, climbing towards the summit of the Cascades, and soon the turquoise water of Diablo Lake comes into view — the vast reservoir nestled among the Cascade Mountains. In all the years she lived on the commune, she only once travelled this side of it, when she left. "Diablo," she says. "Wouldn't it be great if we could put danger warnings on people?" She imagines DIABLO tattooed on Sylvain's forehead. She thinks about how long she harboured love/devotion/fear, how Sylvain loomed so large in her life for so many years. "I wonder whose kid that man is, and whether he even knows who his mother is."

"You don't remember him in the commune?"

"No. There were no children in the commune. Except us girls."

"But there must have been pregnancies," Paris says, frowning. "Unless you were all on birth control…"

"A combination. We all took birth control pills. Sylvain insisted on it. Maybe he was worried the women would be more interested in the children than in him." Skye pauses. "There were a few pregnancies, nonetheless, but none came to term. There was a concoction, something that got rid of pregnancies right away." She pauses again. "Probably for the best. Can you imagine how we would've raised these babies?" She thinks about her volunteer work, and how she and every one of those women could write a sad, heartbreaking memoir.

They drive in silence for a bit, both of them subdued, then Skye says, "I feel bad for that girl."

"That must have been tough," Paris says. "With that man, I mean."

Skye nods, embarrassed by her own complicity. "You don't know the half of it," she says, then proceeds to fill Paris in on the details of her years with Sylvain and Brent, ending with, "So I finally escaped one fire only to leap into another."

"But you had the sense to leave," Paris says.

"Yes," Skye says, "But I left because of Brent, and then served another two years with him. That's how it felt. Like a prison." She pauses. "But I picked them, you know? Or they picked me." She sighs.

"The things we do for love," Paris says.

"Are you and Ferris going out?" Skye says. She's been wanting to ask this for a few weeks, sensing something.

Paris turns, colour rising in her cheeks. "What do you mean?...We've been out a couple of times." She laughs nervously.

"Be careful," Skye says, thinking that Ferris is one of those distant men, just like Paris's father. Those are the ones Paris chooses, as if she were recreating the absent dad, the years of longing, and nothing resolved, though her father's death at least ended it all. Skye wishes her own father was dead.

They coast down the last pass and soon are in Winthrop, a pseudo-frontier-western town of boardwalks and fake fronts. They stop for lattes and home-baked scones, and Skye thinks how fake it all is, this re-creation for tourists. She imagines, for a moment, a re-creation of Sylvain's commune for the benefit of tourists. Whitewashed. Sterile. A rage surges inside her.

"You know what I want to do now that we're here? I want to go and confront Brent." She sits up. "Might as well try to deal with both demons in one trip."

Paris smiles. "Give me co-ordinates."

When she left him, Brent was living on a ranch on the outskirts of Moses Lake, but six years ago, he moved into town, married and had two children in close succession. Skye has kept tabs on Brent out of some perverse wish to see him punished. So far, he appears to be living the model life she imagined for them all those years before. When they stop for a break along the highway, Skye goes online, gets his address, and enters it into her phone's GPS.

Through the rolled-up window, the late-afternoon sun bears down on her, causing small beads of sweat to surface at her brow. The air conditioner has been malfunctioning all afternoon, and they've had to open the windows now and then, which has layered fine red dust over everything. They arrive in Moses Lake in late afternoon, and easily find the house on a cul-de-sac fronted by three identical houses in different colours. A large American flag wilts to one side of the verandah, and on the lawn of the fenced-in yard are a tricycle and a plastic pool. Children's squeals and yelps come from the back of the house. Skye gets out slowly, trying to formulate what words she might say to Brent.

"Call if you need me," Paris says, but she remains in the car.

Skye presses the doorbell and waits until she sees him approach through the wavy glass at the side of the door. He is out-of-focus, unrecognizable.

As soon as he sees her, he quickly steps outside, closes the door behind him, and leans into her. "Skye," he says, and looks her over. "You look good."

She stares at him. He looks filled out. Soft.

He shifts from foot to foot, glancing furtively behind him. "I'm married now," he says. "I've got two kids."

"I didn't come here for that," Skye says, thinking *why didn't he want to marry me?*

"What then?" he asks, relieved. "I mean — look, I'd really appreciate it if you didn't mention anything about…you know…I've turned my life around and…well, I don't need any trouble."

*Trouble.* Is this how he sees her? "Do you have any idea what my life has been like?" she says.

He shrugs. "We all make our choices. We have to live with the bad ones as well as the good ones."

"I didn't have a choice," Skye says harshly.

"Did I kidnap you and take you with me? Did I tie you up and force you to stay?" He glances at the glass panel in the door and lowers his voice to a whisper. "Even at Sylvain's, nobody forced you to do anything."

Rage fires all the synapses of her brain. Brent knew right from wrong. Use from abuse. It seems to her suddenly that abusers can easily "turn their lives around" and carry on, while their victims struggle with indelible scars for the rest of their lives.

"What?" he says.

"You jerk! I was a teenager!"

He shrugs again.

"He ruined my life," she says, "and you— you were—"

"Take some responsibility for yourself, Skye," he says.

She shakes her head and turns away. Storms back to the car, thinking she should charge them both, wondering what the statute of limitations is on sexual assault. For a moment, she fantasizes contacting all the women who've spent time in the commune. They could have their own @MeToo moment, file a class-action suit against Sylvain and Brent.

Paris is consulting the map app on her phone when Skye returns to the car. She sits down, slams the door shut and says, "Well, that's that."

"Do you want to talk about it?" Paris asks.

Skye shakes her head. "Nothing to say. Dead end."

Paris turns the key in the ignition and puts the car in gear. "Are we good to go?"

"Yup."

"I've found a place in Oregon, about three and a half hours away, called Hot Lake. There's a spring there, and we can swim and spend the night. What do you think?"

"Sure," Skye says. She doesn't really care where they stop, her mind still reeling from her exchange with Brent, both angry and afraid that he might be right. When did she abdicate all responsibility for the missteps of her life? How is she to make decisions, if she can't trust herself? She was someone else back then, and someone else before that. She'd renamed herself Eva in Second Life, as a private joke, a nod to *The Three Faces of Eve*, to the three distinct facets of her own life. Perhaps after this, she'll claim that name in her real life.

That night, lying in bed under the flashing red-and-purple neon of the motel sign, Skye thinks about sexual assault versus consensual sex. At the commune, she and the women obeyed Sylvain's rules. And the sex with the commune men — if she were being honest with herself — had been consensual. And certainly all the women had vied for Sylvain's sexual favours, though most of them were underage. Brainwashed. Even their names relinquished. Could they now charge him with assault?

They start out early in the morning to cover the twelve-hour trip to Vegas in one day, switching drivers every three or four hours. They are both silent for much of the journey, exhausted by the inescapable intimacy of the car, each reading or napping as the miles pass beneath their wheels.

In late afternoon, the heat becomes unbearable, the air conditioner still malfunctioning. They open the windows and fan themselves with magazines. Outside, the temperature is over 100 degrees Fahrenheit, and a thunderstorm is imminent.

They arrive in Vegas in early evening, the Strip a river flowing between brilliant hotel signs, blinking lights, five-storey screens projecting dizzying displays. Paris drives and Skye gawks, both astounded and enchanted by the incongruity: high rollers in evening dress walk past homeless men sprawled in doorways; marble arches stand next to kitschy plaster statues. This is the Vegas she has heard about — the epitome of America — where everything good and bad is exposed without shame. Music spills out of every doorway, mixed with the machine-gun rat-at-tat of slot machines, the bass drumbeats of rock bands, the piccolos of laughter. The sidewalks are crammed with tourists in shorts, capris, T-shirts, sandals and runners. She's heard that on the sidewalks, men pass out cards to advertise anything and everything — spas, hookers, shows, restaurants, car rentals, hotels, wedding chapels, divorce lawyers. Whatever one wants, it is available in some form, to suit any budget. This is Vegas, America's Sin City, run by Mormons, frequented by the rich and famous, by the down-and-out, the bored, the gamblers, and everything in between. Monumental hotels mimic tourist destinations: the Eiffel Tower in Paris Las Vegas, the Grand Canals of The Venetian, the Pyramid of Luxor, the man-made lake in front of The Bellagio etc., even the natural world constructed as mountains, volcanoes, lakes and waterfalls. The city a glittering globe Americans can visit without ever leaving their own borders.

Skye understands its allure, the temptation to escape or seek refuge. *Just The Right Amount Of Wrong*, the ads proclaim, because *What Happens In Vegas Stays In Vegas*. Your secrets are safe. Laws don't apply here. That's the problem with secrets, she thinks. *What Happens At Home Stays At Home.*

They continue past Vegas, drive the eighty miles to the Virgin River Hotel and Casino, where they book a room for the night. Skye imagines nymphs in gossamer clothing floating around the hotel. "Honestly," she says to Paris, "I know we're in Mormon territory here, but really, *Virgin*? What century are we in?" She flops onto the bed, and closes her eyes.

Paris picks up the hotel brochure on the coffee table and reads: The Virgin River Hotel/Casino/Bingo is located in Mesquite, Nevada…etc." She scans quickly down the page "700 comfortable hotel rooms … 840 of the very latest slot and video poker games, 17 table games, blah blah." Paris says. "Here's the bit about the name: The river is named for Thomas Virgin, a member of the first American party to see it, led by Jedediah Smith in 1826. There you have it. It has nothing to do with virgins or sex."

"Could have fooled me," Skye says, picks up her cell and enters her parents' address. "It's less than a mile away. We can walk over, then we won't have to worry about drinking and driving."

"Are you sure you want me to come? I'd be perfectly happy here — "

"Please," Skye says. "I'd be a wreck without you."

The next day, in late afternoon, they walk to the house where Skye's parents await in a pink bungalow sprawled in the desert. Flowering bougainvillea spill over a low wall surrounding the property, and within it, lime green, pink, and orange open umbrellas evoke a resort. Music and laughter waft in the air. Skye texts Joe as they arrive, and he comes out to meet them.

"Hey, big sister," he says, easily embracing Skye. "I feel as if I know you already." Then he shakes hands with Paris. "Come in. Come in. Mom and Dad will be thrilled."

Skye's heart thumps in her chest. She turns to Paris, who gives her a reassuring smile.

"Looks like you have a full house," Paris says, eyes twinkling.

"Half the neighbourhood." Joe laughs. "I'm kidding. Thirty or so. Close friends. My wife's family."

Skye and Paris follow Joe into a dim hallway, then a living room furnished with brown plaid couches, then out patio doors, where a crowd swarms, drinks in hand, the men in slacks and button-up shirts, the women in sparkly resort-wear. Skye feels self-conscious in her denim midi skirt and white shirt. On the lawn, large round tables are lily pads on which people set their drinks and mill about. Joe leads her towards the head table, speaking quickly, nervously. "I've told Mom all about you," he says. "I hope you don't mind."

She shakes her head, wondering what exactly he thinks he knows about her, other than what's on her Facebook profile.

As they approach, Skye sees her mother squeezed into a chair, her dress dipping into the space between the trunks of her legs. How she's aged! What did Skye expect? That time would stand still? That she would find the mother of her youth? Her mother sees her and lumbers up. She steadies herself on the table, then picks up a cane and comes towards Skye, one arm open, eyes shiny with tears. "Christina!" her mother says, and Skye flinches at the sound of the name she discarded along with her childhood life. "Oh, how I've dreamed of this moment," her mother says, wrapping her arms around Skye, who lets herself be pressed against the unfamiliar flesh for a moment, then moves out of the embrace.

"Mom," she says.

"Come and say hello to Daddy," her mother says, pulling her through the crowd until they stand next to her father. When he turns, Skye is shocked to see the old man he has become, not the monster she has carried in her head all these years. His thick white hair is combed back from his brow, and his face is gaunt and mapped with grooves. He has shrunk into himself. He peers at her through round black-rimmed glasses. "Is that you, Christina?" he says, and she nods. "It's good to have you home."

*Home.* The world circles in her head, like a Buddhist mantra. Her home was never here.

When her father takes her arm, she feels the familiar sting of his fingers and shrugs him off. He walks her around, introducing her to his friends, as if nothing happened, as if all were normal. Paris follows closely, now and then patting Skye's back.

"This is my prodigal daughter," her father keeps repeating, laughing.

The prodigal son squandered his inheritance in riotous living. The prodigal daughter's inheritance is his scent, the pretence of love and religious devotion. He is the prodigal, who squandered her, who knows nothing about her, has never tried to find her. His hand burns the small of her back. She tries to move out of his orbit; forms her lips into a smile for strangers.

"Dad," she says finally, when they are back at the head table, where her mother anxiously awaits.

"What?" He frowns, his eyes narrowing.

"Christina is living in Vancouver," her mother says quickly. "She does accounts...works for a big company—"

"We need to talk," Skye says, her voice tight, and her mother turns away. Paris herds a nearby couple toward a group of people chatting further along.

Her father reaches for the wine bottle on the table and pours himself a glass. He pauses, the glass still on the table, and she thinks he might say something. Instead, he stares into the crowd, raises his arm and waves at someone. "You're not going to ruin my anniversary," he says harshly, turns and escapes into a sea of friends who part to let him in, then close behind him.

"Asshole," she says, but not loud enough for him to hear.

"Christina." Her mother touches her arm, her tone supplicating. "Let's go inside. Come inside," she says, getting up and pulling on Skye's hand. They weave their way past guests' laughter and children's squeals. When they reach the kitchen, Skye's mother sinks into a chair. "Give your dad a break," she says. "He's worked hard all these years."

Skye stares at her, thinking, what does that mean? How does hard work absolve him? And more importantly, how does his hard work absolve her mother? "You knew," she says slowly. "You knew and did nothing."

"You shouldn't have come," her mother says, her hands trembling. "Everything was finished. We were having a good life."

"A good life," Skye says sarcastically.

Her mother drops her head in her hands. "Why are you doing this to me?"

"This isn't about you," Skye says. "This is about me."

For a moment, they stare at each other. Then her mother leans forward. "You don't know how much I suffered back then. I didn't know what to do." Large tears roll down her cheeks. "I tried to stop him going into your room."

Skye shakes her head. "You didn't try hard enough."

"It was a terrible time for me too," her mother says.

"You should have protected me!" Skye half shouts. A maelstrom rage.

"What's going on here?" Joe is suddenly in the kitchen with them, his voice anxious. "Mom, what's going on?"

"Be careful with your daughter," Skye says. "That's the only reason I came. To warn you."

"I'm sorry," her mother says. "I'm sorry. I didn't know what to do."

Her father now appears in the doorway. He looks from one to the other, weight shuffled leg to leg. Through the open door, sunbeams refract into the room in a geometry of shapes that blind Skye each time he shifts. She shrinks from him, suddenly catapulted into her childhood bedroom. She closes her eyes, feels his weight on the bed, his whispered *shhhhh…shhhhhh.*

Joe's voice returns her to this kitchen. "Why didn't you tell me?"

She opens her eyes. "What for?" Skye says. "You had nothing to do with this. You were a toddler."

"Christina," her father says in the stern voice of her childhood. "It was a different time, a different culture. It didn't seem a terrible thing. I didn't harm you."

*A different time.* Was there ever a time when it was okay for fathers to molest their children? Skye takes a deep breath. "Are you *justifying* what you did?" She leaps across the floor, and slaps his chest repeatedly. "You didn't *harm* me?" She thinks about the capers of her teenage years: the various drugs in her blood, the alcohol on her breath, the high-school suspensions, the bad older boyfriends, the nights she didn't return home. She closes her eyes and sees herself riffle through her mother's purse for money, fold a change of clothes into her backpack, slide open her bedroom window and sneak out. She sees herself walking alone at night, crying out in rage against the sound of her father's footsteps. She feels his arms, Sylvain's arms open like floodgates on Diablo dam to submerge her. "You didn't *harm* me?" she says again, whacking his chest once more. "You didn't *force* me, but you certainly harmed me!"

He flinches, steps back, then looks at her. "I prayed and prayed," he says. "But God — "

"God has nothing to do with this!" Skye says. "Don't you hide behind your god." She pummels his chest again. "I was a child! I loved you!"

The words hang in the air, to the backdrop of her mother's sobs. They are all frozen in place. A trauma diorama.

"I'm sorry," her father says, his voice faltering. "I can't undo the past." He looks stricken. "God deserted me. I'm sorry if… I'm sorry I harmed you."

For a moment Skye doesn't answer, her rage impossible to articulate. She stares at her father, her mother, Joe, thinking *machinations, sham*. A headache forms in the middle of her forehead. She closes her eyes, wills herself not to react, not to give him that satisfaction.

Her father turns, goes into his bedroom and locks the door.

"Now see what you've done!" Skye's mother says. She goes after him, knocks at the door, imploring him to let her in.

Joe stands frozen in disbelief for a moment, then he sighs. "I had no idea," he says. "I would never have pestered you to come if I'd known."

Through the thin walls comes their father's monotone praying voice, which turns into a warbling. Skye holds her breath and listens. "Yes, every secret of my heart / shall shortly be made known," he sings, "and I receive my just dessert / for all that I have done."

Skye lets out a sarcastic laugh. Men like her father, Sylvain, Brent, nameless men everywhere never receive their just desserts. They talk and sing, confess their transgressions, beg forgiveness, and move on. *You're not going to ruin my anniversary*, her father said. Down the hall, her mother continues to plead, and her father remains cloistered, his thin voice rising. She feels herself sinking into childhood, submitting to the ghostly whisper of his voice in the night.

"I'm done here," she says, and pecks Joe on the cheek. "Let's keep in touch." Once outside, she takes a deep breath. She has imagined this confrontation a hundred different ways, all ending with an apology that is supposed to give her "closure," as the therapists and self-help books say. Closure. A guillotine chopping off a past that can't be undone.

She texts Paris and waits, nauseous, lightheaded, her hands like seashells cupped over her ears to contain the whirl of voices, the ocean of ghosts roaring in her head.

# ACKNOWLEDGEMENTS

Some of these stories were written while I was a "permanent tourist" — in Cambodia, Mexico, Thailand, Italy, and the US. Four of them have appeared in print in various journals: "Erasures" in *Prairie Fire*, Summer 2020; "Solitudes" as two separate stories: "Stones" in *Pulp Literature*, Summer 2018, in *Exotic Gothic 2*, Ed. Danel Olson, 2008, and "Water Lover" *Exotic Gothic 4*, (PS Publishing, UK) Ed. D. Olson, June, 2012; "Beached" in *Room*, 35th Anniversary Issue, 35.2 Spring 2012, and in *People Places Passages: an Anthology of Canadian Writing*, Eds. De Gasperi, De Santis, Do Giovanni, (Longbridge Books, 2018). I've used quotations and credits at the beginning of stories and within "Permanent Tourists." My thanks to Danel Olson, editor of the Exotic Gothic series. I am, as always, indebted to Karen Haughian, whose insightful editing, guidance and friendship I value immensely. My thanks to Frank Hook for first reading and everything else.

# ABOUT THE AUTHOR

Genni Gunn, author, musician and translator, has published eleven previous books: three novels – *Solitaria, Tracing Iris* (which was made into the film *The Riverbank)* and *Thrice Upon a Time,* two story collections — *Hungers* and *On the Road,* two poetry collections — *Faceless* and *Mating in Captivity,* a collection of personal essays — *Tracks: Journeys in Time and Place,* the opera libretto *Alternate Visions,* and three translations. Her books have been translated into Dutch and Italian, and have been finalists for major awards: *Solitaria* for the Giller Prize; *Thrice Upon a Time* for the Commonwealth Writers' Prize; *Mating in Captivity* for the Gerald Lampert Poetry Award; *Devour Me Too* for the John Glassco Translation Prize; and *Traveling in the Gait of a Fox* for the Premio Internazionale Diego Valeri for Literary Translation. Before she turned to writing full-time, Genni toured Canada extensively with a variety of bands. She currently lives in Vancouver.